Horse Roghi and
Mr. Money-Man

CAMPBELL SLIMON is the great grand nephew of Robert and Robina Slimon. He is a retired third generation sheep farmer. His son, Archie, now manages the farm. Their hill farm is situated in the middle of the Scottish Highlands and so he appreciates the hardships endured by Icelanders and their way of life.

Other than a scroll and flag presented to Robert by the Icelandic Legislature he was unaware of the eventful and important part that his ancestor had played in Iceland's development. It was only when the eldest of his three daughters, Jean, started research that the story came to light.

He has also written **Stells, Stools, Strupag:** *A personal reminiscence of sheep, shepherding, farming and the social activities of a Highland Parish.* Published by Laggan Heritage, 2007.

The author donates profits from the sale of this book to the Icelandic Farmers Relief Fund.

Horse Kogill and Mr. Money-Man

Campbell Slimon

Grace Note
Publications

Horse Kogill and Mr. Money-Man
paperback edition published by
Grace Note Publications C.I.C.
Grange of Locherlour,
Ochtertyre, PH7 4JS,
Scotland
books@gracenotereading.co.uk
www.gracenotepublications.co.uk

ISBN 978-1-907676-47-5

First published in 2014

A catalogue record for this book is available
from the British Library

Cover design by Alan Davidson
Typesetting by Grace Note Publications

Profits from the sale of this book donated
to the Icelandic Farmers Relief Fund

CONTENTS

ACKNOWLEDGMENTS

There are a number of people, without whose help and knowledge this book would not have appeared.

Firstly, my daughter Jean, who started the whole project and has tirelessly burrowed away finding new material not only on our family ancestry but also with the Icelandic connections. I admit to having no skills in the wonders of computers so in this respect too I have to thank my wife, Sheena, for her unfailing patience and putting up with my clutter.

Olafur Dyrmundsson of the Icelandic Farmers Association has been the most valuable friend with his great knowledge of agriculture and its history and I am much indebted to him for writing the Foreword.

The vast majority of the factual material of Robert Slimon and Capt. John Coghill's careers came from the research of Graeme Somner and to him I owe a great debt.

The travel records of George Sim and Alex Tweedie provided a valuable glimpse at the social life of Icelanders at that time. Bill Holmes provided the prospect of an Emigrant and George Locke of the Sportsman Traveller

The various museums and libraries were without exception most helpful and co-operative with special mention to the Emigration Museum in Hofsos opening up out of season for Sheena and I. They, the National Museum, Akureyri Folk Museum, Reykjavik Museum of Photography and the manor farm and vicarage of Laufas are all in my debt along with Salvar Olafur Baldarsson of Vigur Island. Clive Philips, of 'Brodies', Honorary Consul to Iceland whose vast knowledge of Icelandic horses led him to suggest Thorgeir Gudlaugsson as a valuable contact on the life of Captain John Coghill. and who also supplied the photo. of Capt Coghill on the back cover.

Bjorn Ingalfsson of Grenivik was a valuable contact, as was the Shetland Archives and Reverend Sven Bjarnsson and Katla Arnasdottir very kindly gave of their time to translate various pieces.

Elizabeth Carmichael had the unenviable task of correcting my grammar and spelling. She also made numerous suggestions to improve the text.

FOREWORD

In Iceland the late 19th century goes down in history as a period of hardship, mainly due to low temperatures in several of the years and subsequent poor vegetation growth affecting farming severely. This situation was aggravated by a major volcanic eruption in East-Iceland. One of the consequences was an exodus of people to North-America, mainly from rural areas. My grandparents, born and raised on farms in Northwest-Iceland, told stories of relatives who emigrated and settled in the West. They were missed, this was their new life and few returned.

On the positive side, there were many beneficial developments in the rural communities at this time strengthening their wellbeing and economy. For example, the first agricultural schools were founded, scythes imported from Scotland facilitated mowing and haymaking, all earmark records were printed, and last but not least, the Danish trade monopoly was abolished after the middle of the century and Iceland was gradually reclaiming its sovereignty. The cooperative movement was growing and trade was being liberalized. One of the best known overseas merchants was no doubt Mr. Robert Slimon and he and his agent, Mr. John Coghill, were both respected. They became indeed legendary. Their exports of horses, and particularly of sheep, namely wethers up to four- year old, as many as 30.000 head per autumn spanning over 20 years, were not only a boost to the sheep sector but also of great importance to the national economy in difficult times. This trade certainly contributed substantially to economic growth and prosperity at the time. In 1885 both Slimon and Coghill were officially honoured by Althing, the Parliament of Iceland.

When I first met Campbell and Sheena Slimon in June 2006, together with two colleagues in the Farmers Association of Iceland, I admired their judicious approach in gathering information on the Slimon saga here in Iceland which,from what I have read and heard, is more akin to an adventure than just a historical account. In some respect Mr. Robert Slimon can be regarded as an explorer and a pioneer. Moreover, it was probably uncommon in those days that spouses of foreign visitors would travel with them all the way to a remote island bordering the arctic circle. This Mrs. Slimon certainly did. What a superb way of expanding and illuminating "The Slimon Adventure" – writing a historical novel – where Mrs. Slimon is in charge of the journal !

My congratulations go to the author and the publisher. To those readers who may entertain the idea of following in Mrs. Slimon 's footsteps, in a 21st century way, goes the following message:

Welcome to the Nordic island of ice and fire.

Ólafur R. Dýrmundsson PhD
The Farmers Association
of Iceland, 2013

PROLOGUE

HORSE KOGILL AND MR. MONEY-MAN

So what treasures have you got in your attic? I was brought up in an old draughty farmhouse in the Highlands, where the warmest place was the attic. On cold wet days, this was a place of refuge and peace where as a boy I would examine my fathers collection of birds eggs and butterflies, collected around Edinburgh where he was brought up at the beginning of the twentieth century.

But it was another two nineteenth century items that really caught my boyish imagination. A big blue flag, perhaps seven feet by five feet, with a gyr falcon in attack mode. Attached was a hand written note which stated, "Made by the wives of Reykjavik merchants for Robert Slimon" and with it a beautifully written scroll signed in 1885 by the twenty seven members of the Icelandic Legislature, with their occupations. Speaker, judge, lawyer, doctor and farmer. The Scroll basically thanked Robert Slimon for opening up trade between Scotland and Iceland, which enterprise had benefited the Icelandic people greatly as well as Robert as a businessman. Also, it thanked Captain John Coghill, his agent, for so enthusiastically carrying out this trade with fairness,honesty and vigour.

Iceland was a far distant island of volcanoes, glaciers and geysers. To sail across the wild North Atlantic to a foreign land in small ships with out the navigational aids of today with a cargo of ponies, because that is what we were told was the trade, must have been extremely hazardous and exciting. The ponies being imported for the rapidly expanding coal-mines of the period,

That was all that we knew, other than that Robert was in partnership with his brother, my Great Grandfather David as a ship-chandler in Leith. David had died young, in fact, the same year that my grandfather was born,1869.

It was not until Jean, my daughter, took up residence in 1999 as a community nurse, a few doors along from the long defunct ship-chandlers on The Shore in Leith, that new light was shed on this interesting venture.

Always inquisitive about family history, she started working on the Slimon background tracing back to Carnwath in Lanarkshire in the eighteenth century, via a farm at Gyle outside Corstorphine where Robert is buried.

But it was her discovery of a little book "From England to Iceland" by George Sim, that really set the ball rolling. George recounts his journey to Iceland on board the SS *Camoens* owned by R & D Slimon, his trip on pony trek to Geyser and his journey home with several hundred ponies on board.

The fact that Robert was in the tourist trade and various references in the book suggested that this was a much bigger venture than we had envisaged. It was excuse enough to take a small holiday to this "Island of Adventure".

With my wife, Sheena, our intention was to spend a day in Reykjavik at the National Museum to find out about the flag, the university, in the same campus to enquire about the scroll and hopefully a library. We explained to the girl at reception in the Museum, a wonderful new building, that we had an Icelandic flag and wanted to know its significance. She called for her superiors and when we unfurled the flag, their faces showed utter astonishment. "Where did you get this?" They had a similar flag in the museum , but for foreigners to walk in with what turned out to be an important part of the Museum's history and indeed Iceland's, was a shock to them. The impression they gave us was that this was Iceland's property and therefore should stay in Iceland. The head of the National Museum was out of the country but would be returning in three days time and they would make an appointment for us to meet her.

The story of the flag was that it was designed by 'Sigurdur the painter', also sculptor, a leader of the independence movement and founder of the museum in which we were now standing. By its nature it was very controversial and as it was hand made, there would never have been too many in existence. We had discussed with our family before we left what to do with it as it seemed to us that it should be on display somewhere, so the ideal solution was for us to present it to the Museum.

We were then directed to the appropriate Professor at the University, a short walk away. On explaining who I was, he said "THE Robert Slimon!" He made time in his diary to see us during his lunch hour, when he then explained how important Robert's trade had been to Iceland. Firstly it was not just ponies but much more importantly sheep that he had imported in very large numbers to Scotland. Secondly he had paid in gold and silver, instead of barter, which had the effect of kick-starting the Icelandic economy, for the farmers had then been able to modernise not only their farms but also the fishing industry which was, of course, the big potential wealth creating industry. In addition they were able to afford to send their children to University.

He suggested we meet the President of the Farmers Association and his predecessor, who had been writing a history of Icelandic Agriculture. This was a few days later in the Saga Hotel, not a tourist hotel for visiting parties of geriatrics as I had at first imagined but a five star hotel used by visiting heads of state and royalty. The hotel was owned and leased out by the Farmers Association, but they retained one floor as their offices. We were met not only by the farmers but also the farming press. We were again made aware of how important Robert had been to Iceland but also John Coghill, his agent. It was he who had managed the whole Icelandic part of the operation and had been held in high regard for his honesty and fairness in his dealings. A great character, who was a legend to this day.

However, our hosts had obviously hoped that we would be able to add to their knowledge of this part of their history and we felt we had let them down. So we resolved that we should find out more. We contemplated how we could do this whilst on our revised schedule. Because of the meetings, we now did trips from the Capital and on the last day a flight over the icefields to the northern town of Akureyri.

A few weeks later I phoned a friend whose wife was a folk singer, inviting them to come to a Ceilidh in Laggan. Hugh had an interest in geneaology so I related the story of our trip to Iceland. A few minutes afterwards the phone rang. Hugh had related the tale to his wife, Doris, who had just stared at him in astonishment. Whilst Hugh was on the phone talking to me, she had been reading an article in the 'Scots

Magazine' on Icelandic Pony Trekking in the Pentland Hills. Half of the article was on how Robert Slimon had been the first to import Icelandic ponies in 1870 on a ship called the James & John. How this trade had grown thanks to Captain John Coghill, known as Horse Kogill and the fact that Robert was paying in gold and silver and thus became known as Mr Money-man.

We eventually traced this information to a Graham Somner, who, whilst writing a history on the Port of Leith had written a very full description of the whole Icelandic operation from 1870 through to 1895 when refrigeration and imports from the Antipodes made the trade unviable.

A National Trust of Scotland cruise a couple of years later calling at many of the ports, including the Westmann Islands, that the *Camoens* and other ships had called at seemed a good way of furthering our research and of updating our Icelandic friends in the Museum and Farmers Association.

From what appears to be very humble beginnings in Leith, Robert was employed in the ship chandlers from the age of twelve along with his brother,David. They worked their way up to ownership. Robert acquired the Estate of Whitburgh to the South of Edinburgh where he died in 1896. We are not sure how often Robert visited Iceland, but we do know he took an active part in the day to day organisation of the operation when he was there.

We know that his wife, Robina, visited Iceland on at least one occasion and this is the story of her trip.

Many of the people in the story were actual travellers, sailors and Icelandic residents of the period. I have put words into their mouths, sometimes colourful. No offence is intended and I trust none will be taken.[1]

---

[1]The Appendix at the back of the book contain brief biographies of Robert Slimon and John Coghill along with various statistics concerning the Icelandic agricultural industry and emigration of that period.

CHAPTER 1

A TRAGIC START

It is always hectic in the days leading up to a sailing, but as this was to be my first time with Robert it was doubly so. Everything that the next four weeks' absence could bring about had to be thought of. I had walked the few hundred yards from our home in Wellington Place down to the ship to make sure all our luggage was stowed as I wanted. I had then gone to Robert's office in the family ship-chandlers on The Shore to help him with all the last minute chores when I heard a bit of a commotion in the street outside.

Angus, our self appointed door-man, a retired seaman, spent his days welcoming all our customers with his unfailing Highland courtesy. There was a corrugated tin shack for the night watchman and Angus had commandeered this. But from what I could hear, he appeared to be having difficulty making himself understood. This was not unusual, in that his Barra accent laced with Gaelic confounded even many of the Highlanders that were to be found working in the Leith docks. But this time it was high pitched southern accents. The ladies appeared to be somewhat agitated and I was about to go and see what the trouble was when Angus slowly opened the door.

"I am seenking these fine ladies might like to have a wee word with you, madam. They are looking for teeckets for the *Camoens* and I am after telling them that they get them on the boat. But they are not having it."

"Leave it with me, Angus. Please come in Ladies" I said. " I am Mrs Slimon, how can I help you?"

In the doorway stood two rather agitated, young women, immaculately dressed for Princes Street, perhaps, but certainly not for the Port of Leith sea-front. A busy and bustling industrial scene it was, but its inhabitants were as rough as they come. The only females to be seen, other than fisher-women selling their wares from Musselburgh and washer-women going about their daily chores, appeared in the evening in the seamier parts of the town lurking around the numerous pubs and alley-ways.

"Oh, are we pleased to see another lady? We are booked to sail on the *Camoens* tomorrow and we came to collect our tickets. My brother, who arranged this trip has not returned from sailing off Dunbar and we have just arrived from London on the over-night sleeping car to find him absent from his lodgings". All this was said by the smaller but sturdier of the two young women. Her accent indicated an upper class background.

"I am sure there is no need to worry, madam." I said "There has been a flat calm these last two days, and I imagine he has just been delayed. You'll be Miss Speedie, I presume. I met your brother when he came to book early in the New Year. He struck me as a most knowledgeable and competent young man and I recall thinking that he would be a valuable addition to our journey with his medical knowledge as there are always injuries of one kind or another to attend to. And, yes, as Angus said you get your tickets when you go aboard "

The ladies visibly relaxed and a glow came over Miss Speedie. She was obviously delighted that not only did I assure her that her brother would be on time for the trip but that I had met him and had held him in respect.

I added "Your brother also assured me that he was a very competent rider. This will be very valuable as the Icelandic terrain is trackless and the journey crosses fast rivers and high passes. I shall be accompanying you. I have never been to Iceland. Robert had thought it could be too tough on my own and as you are the first ladies to book, we thought it would be an ideal opportunity. It will be better to face the perils of the journey together."

"Oh, it is wonderful that you are coming too. Vaughan, has told me how tough it will be, but that's why we are coming," she replied. "The London life is making us soft and he reckoned we needed a challenge. I am sure you are right in that he has just been delayed. We depend so much on him. I would not be allowed to go without him

R&D Slimon. Shipchandlers, ironmongers, brass-workers plumbers and tinsmiths. Circa 1910. Author collection.

R&D Slimon Staff. Robert, bald seated fourth front the left. Author collection.

being with me. And, by the way, this is Miss Joan Whyte, a dear friend who is accompanying us on this great adventure. I'm afraid she has no experience of horses but she is a fast learner and she is fluent in German, which will help us communicate with the natives, I believe."

"Excellent" I replied, "pleased to meet you, Miss Whyte. Indeed you are right as the Icelanders are ruled by Denmark and their language while distinctly their own, has a common root with Danish, which in turn is close to German. So it will be most valuable with the guides and the country folk who we will meet."

Miss Whyte gave me a flashing smile as she bent down to pat Sable, who was sniffing the unfamiliar London smells of my visitor. "What breed of dog is this?" she asked shyly. " Its like a big Shetland with a curly tail."

"Sable is an Icelandic sheepdog, sable because of his colour. They are invaluable to Icelandic shepherds as not only do they help with the sheep but will herd the ponies or horses as they call them. When it comes to a river they will jump on the ponies back and cross the river that way."

Now she went down on her hunkers and put her arms around Sables neck "Oh, you clever doggie, Sable" she swooned.

"Perhaps we should go to Granton, where Vaughan moors his boat with the Royal Forth Yacht Club," cut in Miss Speedie, "how far is it and how do we get there?"

"Good idea, its about three miles and you'll get a machine at the bridge over the Water of Leith out there"

"A machine?" she queried.

"Aye, a cab to you, we have some queer words up here.".

"You do indeed " she said with a sideways look at Angus who was re-entering the room with an anxious look on his face. "Thank you very much, we look forward to seeing you tomorrow, Mrs Slimon".

As the unaccustomed waft of perfume was replaced by a draft of cold air, Angus approached the desk. "Och, there's been a terrible accident on the *Camoens*, to be sure. John, the steward, wass coming back on board when the jib of the crane hit him and laid him out. They fear he'll not make it, they have taken him to the hospital."

Robert was out the back organising the transfer of goods to the quayside. So, after asking Angus to tell him, I rushed out of the building and down to the quayside where the *Camoens* was being loaded with all the many provisions required by the Icelanders, from sacks of flour and sugar to rolls of chicken wire and picks and shovels. But all action had come to a halt and groups of men were standing in huddles as I approached. The Captain, Willie Robertson, in charge of the operations on seeing me, extracted himself and came over. He was obviously in a state of shock. Even for a man with long years at sea and many harrowing experiences of ship-wreck and storm you cannot prepare yourself for an incident such as that, that had just occurred.

"What happened,Captain?" I asked putting a comforting hand on his shoulder.

" I am not too sure, I didn't see it myself but they say that John was in a hurry." Willie said with a slight shake in voice.

"You know he always likes a wee dram on his last day ashore and I don't like to say it but he should have been here an hour ago to make sure all his food for the galley was where he wanted it. Anyway, he seemed not to see the crate till it was too late. Jock in the crane is in a hell of a state but poor John, I doot, I doot. It wasnae a bonny sicht."

" Look Willie, I think you should all go down and have your tea break now and I'll have a word with Jock. Here comes Mr Slimon."

My husband and been in the warehouse directing the stores from there to the quayside. Now he was hurrying towards the vessel. Easily recognised with his bald head and long stride among the shuffling hatted workers on the quayside.

Willie ordered the men below and then went to meet Robert. He explained the tragedy again and how it had affected Jock.

"It may sound cruel but the best thing is for him to get back into the crane and finish the job", said Robert. 'The longer he waits the harder it will be. You go and get a cup of tea, man, you look as though you need it and I'll come and have a word with Jock." I followed down into the galley, reckoning that some of the younger members of the crew, who were not much more than boys, would need some mothering.

Whilst I sat down at a table with the group of boys, I could see Robert talking to a clearly shaken Jock. However, after ten minutes or so, his colour had returned and he seemed back to his old effervescent self. Suddenly he stood up.

"Come on boys, there's a job to be finished" and with that he headed for the gangway to be followed by the rest of the crew.

"A word, Willie." The Captain turned and joined Robert as he sat down beside me. " He's a hardy one Jock, he wasn't in the Black Watch for nothing."

"Aye, I was getting worried as to how we were going to finish the job." said Willie.

"But that takes us to the next problem; who do we get as Steward before tomorrow morning?" asked Robert.

"I was thinking aboot that too." answered the Captain. "I don't know of anybody with the experience, who's available at the moment. I am no volunteering to go round the pubs to find somebody."

I intervened. "Your uncle Angus has experience of transatlantic and far-eastern travel and although he is getting on in years, Iceland is hardly a long trip."

"Excellent idea" Robert said, "Going through the passenger list, I am sure they are all fit and seasoned travellers apart from yourself, dear, and the London party."

"Well, I have just met the ladies and they are two spirited young women, so I am sure they won't be a problem and if push comes to shove I would be quite happy to help Angus out. What about it Willie?"

" I never thought I would see the day that Uncle Angus would be under my command." rejoined the captain, "If he's up for it I am O.K.. but just keep the old devil out of my hair."

" Right, I'll go and have a word with him." said Robert "We'll need to get him kitted out from the store. Then I will have to break the news to poor Johns widow. Tell Dave to take over from me in the stores "

So it was that Angus McKinnon, aged,75 but as fit as many half his age,restarted his long career aboard ship, sad though the circumstances were.

CHAPTER 2

EAST COAST AND NEAR DISASTER

I made my way to the *Camoens* not long after day break, to make sure Angus had not got second thoughts about renewing his career. It was a sombre Steward that greeted me and for a moment I feared the worst.

"Good morning, Ma'am, you would not be believing it, but there's been anither terrible tragedy. Last night, a young boy was delivering a passenger to the boat and when he left, going too fast I have no doubt, he went the wrong way and went straight off the quay. Both horse and boy were drowned. He was from the city so he would not be knowing his way about. Anyway there are hot butteries below, Madam, and work to be done" was Angus's greeting as the crane swung a truss of hay over the deck before it disappeared into the hold. This was for the return journey, when the passenger list would include a thousand or so sheep and a few hundred ponies.

"Thank you, Angus. But that is tragic, poor boy. It is time there was proper lighting along the quayside. Perhaps they'll do something now. It always takes a tragedy before anything is done" I said, "My Angus, you look ten years younger in that uniform. Now, don't you be overdoing it. There are plenty of younger folk to share the load including myself."

"Don't you be worrying yourself, Madam, I never felt better. I chust cannot wait till we get under way, otherwise there might be another tragedy. They aye come in threes, or so my mother used to say."

Having assured myself that all was well on the stewarding operation, I busied myself with putting our cabin in an orderly manner. We needed clothes for entertaining, both on board and in Reykjavik, as well as stout material for the expedition to the interior. Whilst Robert also required the strongest materials for assisting with the loading of sheep and horses.

Although we were in the middle of summer, we had to prepare for all seasons as we might get anything from snowstorms and gales to heat-waves.

We had had a few years organising these expeditions and it had been a learning experience for us and our Icelandic guides. But after erring on the side of safety, we took the sound advice of our Icelandic agent, John Coghill, who originated from Caithness. Dress as one would for a trip in our own Highlands, the climate not being too dissimilar. A thick serge dress, short and plain, with a cloth one for change. A tight fitting thick jacket, good macintosh and very warm fur cloak; one pair of high macintosh riding boots (like fisherman's waders) as well as a conventional pair; a yachting cap or a small tight-fitting hat, with a projecting peak to protect the eyes along with blue glasses, from the glare of the ice. Thick gauntlet gloves, flannel shirts and worsted stockings, for sensible wear on deck or in the interior. Even the Icelandic houses could be cold in midsummer, although according to Robert, it was the more modern ones that were not so well insulated. In addition, soft mackintosh 'hold-all' bags suitable for slinging over a pony. Rugs, towels, mackintosh sheets and pillows for camping out. Also towels and all the toilet requisites.

I was taking some provisions, as the food provided would be very basic. I had my own preferences as to tinned soup and meats. White loaves are unobtainable so I would ask the steward to provide bread on departure from Reykjavik. We also took a cooked ham and tongue. Cutlery and tin plates and mugs would also be taken. It was found that wine and whisky were invaluable after a long day in the saddle, not only did it help numb the physical pains of the journey, but also lifted the spirits around the camp fire.

I could hear strange voices aloft, which suggested the passengers were coming on board, so I went up to greet them. We had a very interesting list of people both British and returning Icelanders, so I was looking forward to meeting them. The first duty was to collect the fares. We charged £8 return first class, and £5 second, which included the inland trip, with 6/6d per day extra for food. Every one thought it most reasonable but as one never knew what hardships were ahead of us, it was better to have a happy ship. Also we wanted the Icelanders to think that they were able to travel to Britain, be it for business or pleasure

The S/S *Camoens* of the Leith & Iceland Steam Shipping Company

without financial hardship. They are a very poor people and anything that could help this geographically and climatically disadvantaged nation, Robert would do his utmost to alleviate.

After the apparent chaos of the quayside and yesterday's tragedies, we left right on time. Everybody was on deck as we witnessed a seemingly unavoidable collision which I was certain was going to make Angus's prophesy come true and end our trip before it had even started. A battered old tug, pulling half a dozen mud barges in tow suddenly appeared heading across our bows as we gathered pace going down between the massive sea walls. Just as we think that collision was inevitable she manages, somehow to pull back as we forge past. There is the sound of crashing timber as the barges swing against the side and the sole occupant is dancing up and down pointing at us with clenched fist, shouting abuse, thankfully most of which is lost on the wind and the noise of our engines.

The calm weather of the previous days prevailed and the Forth was like the proverbial millpond. As we sailed over to the Fife coast and looked back to "Auld Reekie" I felt very proud, even as a Leither, to point out the various landmarks of our capital city to our English passengers. The castle on its rock, Salisbury Crags, Calton Hill and the Scott Monument. I was standing next to a Mr Sim, from Bradford, who turned out to be a most interesting traveller and had been to many parts of the globe in his study of geology. "It must be the most beautiful city in the whole world" says he. Certainly, today, with the blue sky, the view was spectacular as we looked away to the east, to the little resorts and fishing ports. Then stretching beyond the coast, the hedge-rowed fields leading up to the Pentland hills. The massive bulk of the Bass Rock, on the starboard bow, white-capped by the centuries of bird droppings, mainly gannets, which some of the passengers with the strongest telescopes, were able to identify.

As we swung north-east, we moved over to the port side to watch the fishing villages of Fife slide by with their uniquely, for Scotland red pantiled roofs.

"I thought you just had these dull grey slate roofs" one of the English ladies said.

"Its a reminder of our close trading links with the Low Countries", I answered. "Scotland traded far more with the Continent than is perhaps realised". I did not want to start a political argument at this early stage of the voyage.

At length, we marvelled at the sight of the Bell Rock lighthouse. The Rock barely visible above the surface, and yet this massive lighthouse was constructed amid the gales and storms. Today it was idyllic, but to work and live in the middle of a storm lashed sea must have required huge strength, courage and skill. Appropriately our bell rang out signalling our first meal on board.

Before saying the grace, Robert made a short speech of welcome. He asked us all to stand, and then offered a prayer and support for the grieving family of the steward. He introduced Angus and encouraged everybody to give him every assistance. He invited anybody with musical or story-telling ability to help pass away the long days. It was only on the last day of a previous voyage that it was realised that an opera singer of renown had been aboard. On being questioned why he never sang, he replied somewhat haughtily that he was never asked.

I had invited the two London ladies to our table as they were obviously new to this type of travel. As I was going with them on the trip to the geysers, I had thought it best that we acquaint ourselves with each other. Their brother, Vaughan, was very much the leader and he engaged with Robert, asking him all about Iceland and its unique landscape of glaciers, geysers and volcanoes, whilst the ladies were more interested as to what the people were like, how they lived and the conditions they would have to suffer. They were obviously used to the highest living that London society could offer and I was concerned that they respect our Icelandic friends with whom we had built up such a good relationship over the years. But for all their airs and graces, they obviously had great spirit.

Angus was in his element organizing his staff of three waitresses who also acted as maids and housekeepers. Their sense of humour and general cheeriness made up for their lack of grace when serving. Our English friends were well travelled on the Continent and used to more sophistication. But they were travellers rather than tourists and as such readily entered into the 'earthy' atmosphere of the voyage. Scotch broth was followed by fresh herring and potatoes and I was relieved to see that this simple fare was enjoyed by everyone. Captain Robertson, whilst not happy with having lady passengers, was too polite to make his feelings known. He felt added responsibility at taking them on a voyage where the odds were that the heavy seas, especially the Pentland Firth, would cause discomfort. He was an excellent raconteur and never appeared flustered whatever the crisis, which is a great gift to have for a ships captain.

We ladies took a turn on deck to breathe in the sea air. Twinkling lights on the distant shore below the glow of the setting sun. It had been a long day and we were sure that even although our beds for the night would be very different to that to what we were used to, we would have no difficulty in having a good nights sleep.

Dawn was breaking when I became aware of the *Camoens* rolling, pitching and heaving. Robert was already on the bridge. Whilst he had total faith in Captain Robertson's judgement, he liked to give him moral support when tricky decisions had to be made. This was such a time. Do we battle on against a near hurricane gale and tide of the Pentland Firth, using up precious fuel or retreat into the shelter of Sinclair Bay and thereby alter the whole timetable, of outward and therefore inward journey? In fact this time, it was an easy decision to make. Such was the strength of the gale that we had no alternative, much to the relief of all the passengers. There were a few empty places in the dining saloon for breakfast, but by mid-morning when we had dropped anchor in the Bay, our new found friends began to appear, some with paint and easel determined to defy Neptune. The Icelandic clothier and her daughter also appeared. The mother with her gaily coloured hat and peacock feather, which had seemed not out of place yesterday when coming aboard, but today with a strong wind even in our shelter, required her to have her hand constantly holding it down. Daughter's face paint showed signs of running down on to her gaudy dress in the slightest shower, in spite of having a huge white hat, which acted as an umbrella. The London ladies were in high spirits,laughing at one another as they tried to keep easels and stools upright and the water in the jars. At one point Miss Speedie toppled right over and remained on the deck helpless with laughter.

By afternoon the storm had abated and when a small fishing boat was spotted making out from Keiss, I suggested they might like to send mail back with the boat. A scramble ensued to get letters written.

"Letters" shouted Angus, but the fishermen shook their heads, considering it too dangerous with the swell, to come close enough. But an hour or so later a bigger smack going out overnight for herring replied "Ay, Ay" and the package,wrapped in a rag, inside a basket was dropped over, accompanied by a bottle of whisky and ten shillings for the crew. The boat shot past on the lee side and cheery waves were exchanged. What hardy handsome men they looked and when they appeared next morning with a parcel of herring, I was awoken by the crews exchanging banter. They were surprised to find us still there and accused Angus of sleeping in and frightened of the Pentland.

"Ach, you don't know what weather iss, boy. Go try feeshing in Uist for a whiley, that'll make a man of you to be sure." was Angus's retort. Word was that it was still stormy ahead and neither of the two bigger boats had moved. One, a large steamer had tried for five hours without success and now had a considerable list and she was still there when we departed after some forty two hours at anchor. But the herring made a welcome addition to our breakfast.

Captain Robertson joined Robert and I at the breakfast table and as we asked for a second jug of coffee, Robert invited Mr Hugh Gordon, and Mr A.L.Thomson, called Al by Mr Gordon and his London female friends to join us. The 'Girls' as he called them, were going on deck to continue their paintings of Noss Head whilst the calm continued. Mr Gordon was an Anglo Indian, on leave from Calcutta for health reasons. Al was a keen sportsman and was regretting missing the 'Glorious Twelfth'.

"You must have had some difficult trips to Iceland, Mr Slimon, " said Mr Gordon, as he poured himself a cup of coffee.

'"Indeed yes" replied Robert. "The Pentland can be the very devil. When you get the tide and wind against you, I'm told it can be the worst in the world. That right Captain?" At that moment Vaughan came below and squeezed in beside his friends.

"Just so, it is not so bad going oot, ye can tak shelter here, but if you hit a Nor Easter comin' home, ye're up against it, for sure" I hoped our guests could understand the Captain's Highland twang. Although Edinburgh born, his parents were from Oban.

."The worst catastrophe we had was the *Copeland*, said Robert. "On her return trip after a flat calm, she ran into a Nor Easter. There were nearly five hundred ponies on board as well as eleven passengers, which included the author, H. Rider Haggard. The gale increased to such strength that she had to reduce to half speed. Part of the problem was that Captain Thomson couldn't close the hatches as otherwise the horses would suffocate. The steering gear had to be reinforced to keep her head into the wind. The vessel was shaken from stem to stern by huge waves and whilst the conditions were fearful for the passengers which included an Icelandic woman with baby, it was much worse for the poor ponies enduring day after day soaked by the seas breaking over them. They were frightened by the noise and thrown about by the violent motion. The result of which, the weaker ones fell and succumbed. Fifteen were lost in this way. Four days out, the storm started to abate and the Captain tried to make headway, but such was the force that the ship was being shaken to bits. The man on the helm was thrown over the wheel three times by the force of the sea on the rudder.

By midday the storm had abated and a course was set for the Pentland Firth. By the time she reached Thurso a thick fog had descended and normally she would have dropped anchor until the fog lifted, but they were already five days out on a journey that took three and a half days and they had only one feed of hay left for the ponies. Leith was still twenty hours steaming away.

Captain Thomson had thought he had passed the Isle of Stroma and altered course slowly to the South. In the thick fog, unfortunately, he had altered course two minutes too early. He saw white breakers on rocks ahead, immediately rang for the engine to be put full astern. Although he was only running at half speed, he could not prevent her from hitting the rocks. It was Rider Haggard who described the chaos that ensued. Everybody was thrown about, the firemen raking out the boilers, the crew trying to assess the damage. Luckily there were few passengers. On the two previous sailings there had been several hundred emigrants, many of them, women and children and a heavy loss of life would have been inevitable. The *Copelands* plight had been observed from the shore and boats had been put out. An islander climbed on board and advised immediate evacuation as the boat was sitting on sixty fathoms of water under her stern. "Get off quickly, for Gods sake, there's five feet of water in the hold. She's only hanging on the rock." A rope ladder was put over the side and everybody climbed into the islanders boats, as the ships ones had become fast due to the storm. It was only when it was thought that everybody was aboard that they realised that the Icelandic lady and her baby had been left behind. She had been hiding in the smoking room ever since the storm had struck. A crew member rushed back on board and retrieved them.

About one hundred and twenty ponies were pushed off the deck by the crew and two of the passengers who were also buyers. They all swam to the rocky shore a hundred yards distant. Unfortunately the poor brutes in the hold were drowned.

On the island, they were taken to a house and given warm food and drink.. It was then suggested that they be rowed over to the mainland at John o'Groats, where it was only seventeen miles from the town of Wick. From there they could catch a train to the South.

The passengers were not encouraged by a crew member who queried why there was no food and drink being taken as they could be swept away by the current and might be adrift for days. Apparently this had happened before, but the Stroma men obviously knew the conditions and were able to reassure everybody that there was no danger. They climbed ashore not much more than two hours later and on the road to Wick and thence to Edinburgh by train."

"And The *Copeland*?", queried Vaughan"

"Yes, well I'm afraid she did slip off the rocks and disappeared. A big loss" answered Robert.

"Well that's some story" said Vaughan. "They were lucky to have been seen by the people on the shore. Especially as there was dense fog."

"That's right, apparently it was children playing on the shore that raised the alarm," said Robert. "We might have lost everybody and no-one would have known what had happened."

"You've sailed the seven seas, Captain Robertson, have you had any experiences like that?" asked Mr Gordon.

"I've had a few in my time, thats for sure." replied the Captain. "Thiss boat hass had a scrape in the Pentland herself, aye and a scrape it wass."

"I think you are trying to scare us from proceeding any further" said Vaughan, "What happened?"

"Well now, let me see" The Captain looked out of the porthole a while, took a long draw on his pipe and started pacing about the saloon. "It wass the year after the ice. That right, Mr Slimon?"

"Yes" said Robert "We had a bad year with the *Camoens* being damaged by ice with seventy emigrants on board, up in one of the North Eastern fjords. She was beached and her plates repaired but delayed for ten days. We had been unable to get to the North of Iceland because of ice until late in the season. There was an increase of emigrants as many feared they would be unable to survive another winter. Their stock were in poor condition and with no spring they would be unable to make much hay for the approaching winter. Remember the previous year had been very late as well. We landed over seven hundred emigrants at Granton that summer."

"Granton?," queried Al "Where is that and where were they going to, these poor folk?" asked Al.

"I am sorry. Granton is a couple of miles up the coast from Leith and their final destination was Western Canada, Winnipeg, Manitoba mostly" replied Robert. "We are agents to the Allan Line, so we just put them on a train at Leith for Glasgow or Liverpool. Then to Halifax or Montreal. Then by train across the prairies."

"It is an awful journey", I added, " especially for the old folk and young women with babies, remember they were half starved before they even set out. Anyway, I'm sorry, carry on Captain"

"Well now," said the Captain. "The *Camoens* wass on her outward journey when did she not hit the rocks in thick fog off Bruneness in the Orkneys. She lost her rudder and the tug the *Iron King* from Dundee towed her to Scapa Flow for temporary repairs and then to the dry dock in Granton. Then dash me if Captain Sutherland doesn't go and run aground off Rosehearty in mid-October, with the *Craigforth* and over sree sousand sheep and a puckle ponies. The crew were all safe, but seex hundred sheep were lost. The Captain lost his certeeficate for sree months after the enquiry. They said he hadn't allowed for the set of the tide. Never mind, I had a great trip through the Mediterranean, with the *Camoens* the next Spring. No ice there, for sure. Nothing but Spanish senoritas and the Italian lassies are no bad either. But here, when I got back, had the Boss" and here he points his pipe at Robert, "not got this wild scheme to tow a barge all the way to Reykjavik with a sousand tons of coal and lime and corrugated iron and God knows what else. I said you must be daft but no he inseested and I have to say this wee boat did it with no bother. Mind you if we had a storm like what we are having chust now, I am not so sure, but here, here, its time I was back on the breedge and weighing anchor." With that he disappeared up the ladder with surprising dexterity for such a big man.

"Aye, that was a wee bit risky," said Robert. "But it made such a difference having a supply of coal sitting in the barge. It meant we could take more cargo instead of coal on the outward journey."

"It seems to have been exciting times for you, Mr Slimon, but not without great financial risk, I would imagine," said Vaughan. "I am sure I read in the "Scotsman" that Leith had honoured you with a reception for all the benefits that you had brought to the Port. That you had greatly expanded the ship-chandlers and there-bye, presumably giving more employment. How long have you been with the firm?"

"It has been my whole life, I started work with the firm when I was twelve in 1840. I was brought up on the farm of South Gyle beyond Corstorphine. Along with brother David, we worked our way up and the opportunity arose for us to take over. At that time it was just a ship-chandlers but we were asked if we were interested in purchasing wrecks. We could sell the timbers and fittings through the firm which helped with the cost of refitting the vessels. In this manner we started trading with these boats and at the same time acquired premises for joinery and other metal works and storage. With the increase of leisure travel we found, too, an increasing demand for more household items like carpets, curtains and bathroom fittings.

But I suppose it was when a previous contact, William Gunn, a salvage expert, who asked us to consider refitting the *Louise*, that our trading exploits seriously started. That was in 1870. We went into partnership with him and we renamed it the *Yarrow*. Previously we had salvaged three or four eighty foot wooden schooners but the *Yarrow* was double the length, a seventy-five horse power iron screw steamer. William had imported a few Icelandic ponies himself and to make use of the *Yarrow's* capacity this proposition seemed to have potential . We already had experience of importing ponies from Germany, as I had a licence. But the competition there was very strong. Iceland was virtually untapped and of course, they had tens of thousands of ponies and the political climate was very favourable. The big risk was the journey, the long winters and lack of loading facilities in what in fact is a much bigger island than many people realise. How big do you think it is in relation to England, Scotland, Wales or Ireland?"

"Before you asked the question I would have said the size of`Wales, but presumably it must be bigger." offered Al.

"It is the same shape as Ireland, but it wont be as big." stated Vaughan.

"You are closer than one of my relations who thought it would be no bigger than Skye. In fact, Ireland is about thirty thousand square miles, Iceland is thirty eight."

"Really, that is very surprising." said Vaughan. "So what is the population?"

"About 70,000," replied Robert. "They are all round the coastal fringes with very few inland, as a high percentage of the interior is glacier or lava beds. I have to say even with the information gleaned from William Gunn and others, it was still a much bigger challenge than expected. Without John Coghill's expertise as sailor, farmer and dealer, we would never have had the success that we have had. The ponies themselves seemed to be ideal for the pits being docile, hardy and tough. A number are also used for children, learning to ride, for which they are ideal."[1]

"This will be the famous Horse Coghill that I have read about," said Vaughan.

"Yes, a great character. You will meet him in Reykjavik." said Robert. "He is scheduled to be there for the return journey. He it was that took our few first ponies home on the *John and James* but it was mainly fish. However, on the second trip, having made contacts, he brought back about seventy ponies, in the meantime the *Yarrow* made two trips with over three hundred on each."

"And what part does your brother, David play? Is he at home looking after the shop?" asked George.

George always had his notebook in hand and I felt he could be too inquisitive, but Robert seemed not to mind

"Unfortunately in 1869 he got rheumatic fever and after a month it developed into pericarditis. He died at his home out at Cramond to the West of Edinburgh. He was just thirty nine. Most unfortunate, in that it was the same year that his only son, William, was born."

---

[1] See Appendix 2 Capt. John Coghill.

"Oh, I am sorry," said an embarrassed George

He was interrupted by excited shouts from above. A twenty five foot long bottle-nosed whale with two porpoises in tow were sporting themselves right around the ship. Some of the ladies were trying to sketch them, which was causing great excitement and hilarity as they rushed from side to side. Of course, the first sighting always causes great excitement, but as the journey progressed and the sightings increased, so the passengers remained at whatever pastime they were indulged in, when the cry of "Thar she blows" was made.

We got underway at noon heading for John o' Groats and the Pentland Firth.

CHAPTER 3

A NIGHT OF STRANGE HAPPENINGS

What a disappointment John o' Groats proved to be. A ghastly pretentious modern hotel of the Scottish baronial style deposited in this desolate landscape, with seabirds of all description wheeling and diving. As telescopes were focussed on the building, discussion ensued as to who was John o' Groat or John de Grout. One suggestion was that he was merely mythical, others that he was named so because he offered to ferry across the Firth for a groat, that is four-pence. No, said someone else, he was a Dutchman who had eight stalwart sons who each demanded to be at the head of the table. So the father got an octagonal table made to keep the peace.

Whilst our passage through the Pentland Firth was by no means pleasant, there was low cloud which prevented us from viewing the spectacularly rugged coastlines of the North coast and that of Orkney. However, the seabirds thrilled our passengers. Never had they seen so many. Gannets diving. Guillemots, arctic terns, kittiwakes and storm petrels were all identified as well as my favourite, the puffin.

When I pointed and said, "There's a bonxie". I began to feel quite an expert.

"A what? Ah, you mean an auk, Robina" said Vaughan, "That's what they call them in Orkney too. I heard tell of them from Dr Rae, a friend of fathers. Dirty brutes are they not?"

"Yes" I explained "They kill young birds and will attack you if they get the chance."

"Tell me, Vaughan, thats not Dr John Rae, the explorer?" interjected Robert. "He lives in Orkney."

"Yes, the very same." replied Vaughan, "He certainly caused a stir in London when he returned with evidence of finding remains of Sir John Franklin's expedition in the North-West Passage."

"I heard all about it," said Robert. "He was in Iceland many years ago. I have a high regard for him. He respected the Eskimos and they respected him. So different from Franklin, whose attitude was that they were just ignorant savages, albeit that they manage to live in such a hostile climate."

"I know he was in Iceland" put in Miss Speedie "When we were deciding whether to come on this trip or not, we asked his advice. He suggested the expedition that we are planning to the interior would be too tough for women."

"But, you came anyway?" said Robert.

"Alex's tougher than many a man, I can assure you" said Vaughan.

"I am sure she is." said Robert. "I would not be letting Robina go if I had thought she couldn't manage. You'll find the Icelandic women very kind and helpful but they will be a bit surprised when you knock on their door. They have seen very few women from other countries, certainly those who live away from the coast."

Our evening meal conversation was dominated by Dr Rae's heroic exploits. Ornithology, was also under discussion with some of our artists keen to enhance the pen sketches they had made of the birds. I must say I was most impressed by their enthusiasm and their talent. The deck of a pitching ship is not the best studio one could think of.

Miss Speedie described how she was just finishing her painting of Noss Head when a speck of soot from the funnel landed on her 'beautiful sea'. So she improvised by turning the smudge into a fishing smack. "I had to make the boat look uncared for, but now I think it has added to the composition and an improvement on the original." she said gleefully.

After taking a turn on deck to view the setting sun, the first we had seen of it for three days, we retired to our bunks in a happy frame of mind.

" What the hell's going on" said Robert as we were both wakened by a stramash above us. He swung out of the bunk and pulled on his trousers all in one action and was up on deck in seconds. The boat's engine seemed to have stopped and started up again. My immediate thought was that we had hit something, but as we were well clear of land my thoughts turned to ice. Surely not as far South as this. I hurriedly got dressed and was just about to open the cabin door, when Robert re-entered.

"Robina, you had better come. Ewan has taken a turn and jumped overboard. If we get him back he will need looking after."

Ewan was the youngest of the crew, a likable young man, extremely polite and keen on his job. He could be highly entertaining, dancing hornpipes and singing at the same time. But also, he could go into himself and be moody and take any criticism to heart. The Captain had taken him under his wing because the crew could be quite cruel. He liked nothing better than being at the wheel and was very competent.

Ewan had been at the wheel when suddenly he had started shouting and rushing about. He grabbed two mops which he had intended to use as oars and jumped overboard. Captain Robertson always gave the impression of being very casual but when it came to a crisis, it was as if he took on a different personality. The whole crew were assembled, a boat lowered and the ship was now in reverse.

There were no shortage of volunteers. Ewan was just visible in the half light appearing and disappearing between the troughs. When the boat with two strong rowers pulled alongside, Ewan redoubled his efforts and swam faster. It is hard enough to pull a man on board, but doubly so when the man is fighting against you. It looked as if the rescue was going to fail, the sailors were soaked and cold. The Captain shouted words of encouragement to redouble their efforts to pull Ewan aboard. At the same time, cold and tiredness set in and he was hauled into the boat unconscious and then hoisted onto the deck. We stripped him of his clothes and took him into the warmth of the saloon, wrapped in a blanket. He started to shiver violently. The crew took it turns to rub him. It seemed like an age but would have been perhaps half an hour before we could see that we were winning. We sat him up and he took a plate of soup and then he started to rant. He seemed to think that the captain had planned putting him into the boiler. A conference ensued as to what should be done.

There seemed no alternative than to lock Ewan up. Also, he would have to have a warden, in case he did damage to himself, when from time to time he became obstreperous. This effectively meant that the crew would be cut by two. "We'll be scrubbing the decks by the end of this trip." said Robert as we descended again to our cabin. Angus was finding the going tough as the steward. There were long days and more than once he had to be raised from his afternoon nap.

For the rest of the trip Ewan had to have a close guard. Once he tried to escape his prison by going through a ventilation shaft and it was only with great difficulty that he was extracted. There were times of violence, times of moody silence and occasionally he was in high spirits, when he was allowed on deck he performed hornpipes and sang sea-shanties to his hearts content. Vaughan attended the patient daily, for which we were very grateful. Captain Robertson blamed his sudden illness on the phase of the moon.

The next day the events of the night were gone over and our passengers were united in praise of the heroism of those who carried out the successful rescue. The crew was justly proud of its achievement. At midday Robert gathered everyone on deck and made a short speech thanking the crew for the nights events, putting there own lives at risk.

The next night we passed the Faroes on the starboard. We were behind schedule and we pushed on with full sail, as luckily the wind was with us and we were making ten knots. Not a ship did we see as the Atlantic breakers washed over the deck. Our deck chairs slewed about, so we lashed ourselves to the railing. This was preferable to the stuffy atmosphere of the saloon. The only excitement was the spouting of whales.

Late afternoon the sea became calmer and I was just nodding off when there was a jubilant shout of "Land Ahoy!"

I had not expected the Icelandic coastline to be so dramatic. But as we steadily neared Iceland, rugged snow capped mountains grew along the horizon, a forbidding looking country. A growing sense of excitement grew as the artists went to work capturing first impressions. Vaughan, Speedie and George Sim erected their cameras discussing the various aspects of this wonderful new invention.

CHAPTER 4

AKUREYRI AND ICELANDIC HORSES

Midnight saw us inside the Arctic circle, with everyone on deck. A toast was drunk to Neptune, as we crossed the mythical line and indeed to many others as we sailed past the Island of Grimsay on the starboard bow. It was one of these magical moments when one feels privileged to be alive. The sun low over the Western horizon, reflecting off Iceland's snow capped mountains in various shades of orange. The sea had the merest shimmer, so that a whale blowing a mile or so ahead was clearly visible. Miss Alex had a knot of admirers round her easel as she recorded the occasion. Robert and I bade everyone good night as tomorrow would be a busy day with much business to be done.

By morning we were moored to a pier in Akureyri with a large building proudly flying the Danish flag. A few years previously we would not have been able to trade with the Icelanders as the Danes had a monopoly but a movement led to Home Rule being granted in 1874. This was led by Mr Sugersson, known as the Liberator of Iceland. His untiring efforts and powerful eloquence are universally acknowledged and he is regarded as a modern day hero by a grateful nation. But there is still a strong loyalty to Denmark and we suspected the flag was flown for our benefit.

We were going to be a day here whilst cargo was first offloaded and sold to the locals already gathered on the pier. I must say I had mixed feelings as we witnessed the poverty of these people and the reaction to obtaining some of what we have come to regard as the most basic necessities of life. It seemed the whole population, including women and children had turned out, if not to buy then to witness the event. All the goods had been piled in a semi-circle, with the auctioneer sitting at a table in the middle. He was assisted by two or three obviously senior locals.

Beyond the populace were the ponies. An amazing sight to see. Not just the number of them, but how they all stood patiently for hours on end. Some with their foals, a few of which would have to be strapped to their mothers back as the journey back home would be too much. Fine sturdy little animals they are, from eleven to thirteen hands high. They had good hind-quarters, thick necks, well shaped heads and tremendously bushy manes. Their feet and fetlocks were not unsurprisingly good as well, as otherwise they would not be able to undertake the long journeys over treacherous terrain. They were black, brown, white, chestnut and piebald. The pack ponies are never groomed, whilst the riding ones were housed and in better condition. They had all manner of saddle or pack. Some were almost hidden from view by the size of the sacks they were carrying.

Robert explained the procedure. Much of the sales were done by barter, but as soon as a deal was sealed, the ships crew, with the help of an interpreter, exchanged the goods or money. Flour, sugar and salt took the highest priority and thankfully there seemed ample for everybody. Coffee was highly valued and as we were to find out later the Icelanders are great drinkers of that brew. Spirits, wines and tobacco were also much sought after and there was some banter as to what prices were being paid, but generally this was a serious occasion.

Robert, who had been moving amongst some of the farmers, observed that he could see a marked difference in their well-being. They were now able to afford some of the more luxurious goods such as stylish clothing and jewellery. I could feel that he was thrilled by this for he has developed a strong attachment to this nation. They have had a long history of deprivation and extreme hardship. Robert has, with the help of John Coghill, our agent, improved the lot of these people and generally given them a greater sense of purpose.

A tall distinguished man had appeared amongst the now slowly diminishing crowd and started to wave. I realised that he was trying to attract Roberts attention. "Ah, its William Stephansson." said Robert "Come over and I will introduce you."

I had heard about this gentleman, as he was one of the chief officials in the area. He grasped Robert round the middle and kissed him on both cheeks. I had seen the Icelanders greeting each other in similar manner, but had not quite expected my husband to be greeted so enthusiastically. I was accorded similar treatment when introduced.

"We were expecting you a couple of days ago. I expect these gales held you up?" asked Mr Stephansson.

" Yes." replied Robert. "We had to hove to in Sinclair Bay for a day and a half. I hope these folk weren't put about too much."

"Not at all," said Mr Stephansson, "They are well pleased with their trade which compensates for any inconvenience. Its a small holiday for them meeting up with friends and its a change for some of the children to see the sea. Now would you like to come along to my humble abode. We are really pleased with our rhubarb this year and my wife is dying to show it off."

" That would be wonderful." said I, "I am dying to stretch my legs. One gets so lazy on board with nothing much to do bar eat and talk."

It was a good half a mile into the town. On the way we pass a large building, the odour of which we could detect from the boat. This was the shark oil manufacturing plant. William explained that this was a valuable export of Iceland mainly to Denmark for the manufacture of soap. There was not much going on today as the workers would have been along at the pier making purchases. But there were three large cauldrons of shark livers simmering away, the liquid being thick and dirty looking. The shark known as the "Squabus Borealis" is up to eighteen or twenty foot long. It can be eaten, but it is only the liver that is used to make oil. Five to fifty gallons per fish can be obtained.

The schooners used are up to fifty tons and manned by eight to ten men. In winter the fish are found in shallow water near the shore, perhaps just twenty miles off shore, and no more than fifty fathoms in depth. In summer the sharks are much further out. The hooks used are twelve to eighteen inches long and baited with horseflesh or whale blubber. They are attached to the end of the line, which is one and a half inches in diameter. Two yards of chain are attached and drawn up to two fathoms from the bottom. On being brought to the surface the shark is then attacked with harpoons and lances. There are incentives for the captain and crew for each barrel of oil.

"Now what do you think of that?" asked Mr Stephansson. For a moment I could not see what he was meaning, but then I remembered that Akureyri possessed the only three trees in Iceland and here was one of them. A very ordinary rowan or mountain ash stood at the side of the road. "I know Scotland is covered with trees but we are very proud of these." He was pointing to another two further up the slope behind a house.

"Magnificent" said I, "How do they survive some of the winters you have had of late?"

"Well, if they can survive perhaps we should be trying harder to find other species that will also stand up to the climate. Is the rowan your hardiest?" asked William.

"I am not a botanist" I replied " but the birch once established would be just as hardy I would have thought. The Scots pine or Norwegian spruce being conifer would give lots of shelter."

We were now in the town and Mr Stephenson pointed out the new hotel built with freshly painted weatherboard. It was a bright yellow. I couldn't help but contrast it and the other gaily painted buildings with our own drab grey stone back in Scotland and remarked so. William seemed pleased. He had been to Denmark and Norway and Icelanders generally followed their Scandinavian cousins.

As we were passing a building which declared itself as the Sheriffs Office, a fit young man coming out almost collided with us.

"Hi, William," said he. "Just been paying my fine and it has been well worth it. I am sure I got as much back from the good Sheriff in the form of refreshment."

"This is Andrew Buchan, scientist, ornithologist, hunter and much more besides." introduced Mr Steffansson. "Andrew, Mr and Mrs Robert Slimon, newly arrived on their ship the 'Camoens'.

 "Ah! Very pleased to meet you. I have the pleasure of sailing with you to Reykjavik in a couple of days." replied Andrew.

"Look," said William". We are just on our way to have a coffee in my house. You look as if you need one too. Why don't you join us and tell us what mischief you've been getting up to."

"Good idea," stammered Andrew, "A very good idea. By hell, he pours a big one, the Sheriff."

We admired William's rhubarb patch, which was indeed impressive, taking up half of his front garden but now past its best. For some reason rhubarb seems to grow particularly well in this Northern clime. Mrs

Steffanson came out of the house, a substantial two storey weatherboard building, again freshly painted a deep green. She bent down and pulled a stalk and offered it to me to sample. I have to say it seemed to have more taste than ours at home and said so.

"Ah, that's our horse dung. Thats what makes the difference." said William.

"Very good, I'm sure", said Andrew. "Now where's that coffee, Mrs Steffanson? You make the best coffee in Iceland and thats saying something, and am I needing it today? Ah, but he's a good man the Sheriff!"

After settling down with our coffee and Mrs Steffanson's scrumptious cake, Andrew explained the reason for his visit to the Sheriff.

"I shot a brace of willow grouse and a redshank for my research without permission and quite rightly I was fined. Its an interesting fact that the redshank is one of the birds that is noticeably bigger than the British variety. Probably because of the harsher climate they have to be bigger and stronger to survive. The Sheriff was more concerned about the grouse, partly because it is traditionally the main dish of the Icelandic Christmas dinner and partly because there has been a great increase in foreigners coming to shoot just for sport, and while these people are very beneficial to our economy, we have to look to the long-term and make sure we do not deplete our resource."

"Now,in the same way" said Mr Steffanson getting up and going into a glass fronted case for glasses, "You, Mr Slimon, have taken thousands of our sheep and horses,but you and the redoubtable John Coghill have always stressed that you just take what is surplus to requirements. John's stocksmanship and integrity as a dealer has, without doubt increased the quality of horse and sheep and indeed the stocksmen, over the last couple of decades. We are now seeing a new sense of pride in the farmers , especially the younger generation. John is a bit of a hero to these young men and dare I say women! So much so that I would like to propose a toast". By this time he had charged our glasses. " To our Scottish Friends. May our friendship continue to prosper."

I got the sense that Mr Steffanson's well documented hospitality was just beginning, so hastily reminded Robert that I had promised Miss Speedie that we would go and see their party off to the waterfall, a local attraction. They had been greatly excited about the prospect of riding the Icelandic horses.

Robert was, I think, grateful of my intervention and seconded my wish especially as he had business to attend to with some of the local merchants. We thanked our hosts for their hospitality and could see a party of horses and riders in the street below us.

There seemed to be a bit of confusion as we approached. Andrew seeing that there was language difficulties stepped in and offered to act as interpreter. This was gladly accepted.

Some Icelandic women ride their horses astride, as in fact do most women throughout the world. Others side-saddle, using an odd chair-like saddle. In England it is still regarded as most unladylike to ride astride. We were told there was an adequate supply of ladies saddles in Reykjavik but not here in Akureyri, where there had been little demand. Miss Speedie and her friend were insisting that they ride side saddle and someone had been despatched to find one. This gave us a chance to study the little crowd who had gathered to view this unusual happening.

"They all looked so dejected" said Miss Speedie, "Is it their hard living or the lack of sun that makes them so despondent looking?"

"They undoubtedly have a hard life, often near starvation," I said. "And no doubt the lack of sun gives them a sallow complexion, but Robert assures that when you get to know them, there are no kinder people and with a pawky sense of humour."

There were two or three pretty lassies, fair hair, blue eyes and with clear skin. Their hair was in long plaits, turned up, forming two loops crossed on the crown of the head. These braids had quaint little black silk knitted caps, fitted close to the skull like an inverted saucer and secured to the head by silver pins. Hanging from the cap is a thick black silk tassel, six or more inches long, which at the top passes through a silver tube, of fine craftsmanship.

Miss Speedie was determined to purchase one. I thought she might acquire them cheaper in Reykjavik, but did not say so, as I knew these folk needed all the help they could get.

Eventually two saddles appeared, they were more like chairs. With more than a little difficulty, Miss Speedie and Miss Joan mounted.

"We will go down the street and back to see how we go. The ground is quite smooth." shouted Miss Speedie to us.

Off they went but not far. The saddle slipped off her horse. Vaughan assisted by tightening the girths and they eventually arrived at the bottom of the street. Miss Speedie dismounted and even from our distance we could see there was a heated discussion. Miss Speedie pulled the saddle off and with Vaughan's help remounted, this time, sitting astride. Vaughan helped to adjust her skirts, then they started walking but half way up she had broken into a trot. By the time she drew up beside us she had a huge grin on her face.

"That's it. This is the way to ride these animals. Its far more comfortable. Come on now, Miss Joan. Throw away that saddle and up you get." Miss Joan, not being a horsewoman, was a bit wary but did as she was bid. Vaughan having got her dress in order, she walked round in a little circle. From being obviously nervous and holding tight, one could see her visibly relax.

"Oh, this is much better. I feel more in control. I am sure the pony, sorry horse, is more comfortable too. Thanks Vaughan for your help."

Then to the Icelandic guide Miss Speedie said. "Sorry to keep you waiting. Let's get cracking and see this waterfall."

Off they went waving cheerily. Miss Speedie was already breaking into a trot obviously enjoying herself. She seemed to be a bit of a rebel and I am sure she was already thinking of what she would tell her friends back in London. Of how she had ridden astride and how they would react.

"Mrs Slimon."

I turned to see George Sim, our geologist and world traveller. "I say, these ladies have spirit, haven't they. I believe you know Mr Stephansson," said George. "I wonder if you could give me an introduction. Coming from Bradford, I have more than a passing interest in wool. At present the Danes buy it and then transport it via Copenhagen to Bradford. It would make sense for the Icelanders to have it shipped directly to Leith or Newcastle, then to Bradford. I believe Mr Steffanson is a man of influence."

"Surely, but we'll have to hurry to catch him." I said, "I think he was planning to go out."

"I haven't seen many sheep as yet" said George, as we ascended the hill again. "But I believe they are descended from our Northern breeds Cheviot, Shetland, Soay and Norwegian. So I presume although the

Danish traders buildings in Akureyri flying the Danish flag, indicating their authority. Source. Used by permission of the Akureyri Folk Museum (AFM).

One of three trees said to grow in Akureyri and indeed Iceland in the 19th century. Used by permission of the Akureyri Folk Museum (AFM).

Bourgoisee enjoying their rhubarb patch. Rhubarb was extremely valuable as it was the first 'green' food to be available after the long winter. Used by permission of the Akureyri Folk Museum.

fleece is only maybe one and a half pounds or so, it is very fine and therefore of great value."

"I think you are right, and it makes obvious sense to ship it direct, but the Danes have a great deal of influence still. Here, this is a steep hill. You soon get unfit sitting about in the boat all day. Ah, here we are now. I see his boots and hat still in the porch, so you are in luck."

Mr Steffanson had seen us coming and opened the door. "Another cup of coffee or is it the rhubarb you are after, Mrs Slimon?" he said, with a big grin.

" Oh no thank you." I said. "This is George Sim from Bradford. He is one of our passengers and he would like a word with you on the thorny subject of wool. I shall leave you with him. I must go to the apothecary before he closes at mid-day."

The apothecary was obviously the meeting place of the town. Little groups stood about outside discussing the topics of the day, the main one of which seemed to be the arrival of the *Camoens* and the cargo it had brought. Inside, I had difficulty making my way to the counter and nobody seemed in much of a hurry.

Some of the customers were from the *Camoens*, both passengers and crew and there was a good buzz between locals and visitors. There were hand knitted gloves and other locally made garments, which were selling at what seemed to me to be rather expensive prices. The gloves were odd in that when worn on one side they could be turned over and put on back to front as it were.

Angus, our steward, was in conversation with as pretty a young Icelander as I had seen and whose English seemed somewhat better than Angus's.

"Now, Angus, is this you chatting up the girls again." I said. They both had their fists clenched in front of them.

"Ye ken, Mrs Slimon, this bonny lassie has been teaching me how to remember the days in the month." said Angus. "Put your fists out like that and I'll show you. Now" pointing at the knuckle on my left. "January 31, February in the hollow, the next knuckle, March 31, hollow, May 31 and so on. All your knuckles are months with 31, richt tae December. Is that nae clever?

"Indeed it is." I said. "I shall have to teach that one back home." The girl smiled at me, obviously pleased that she had been able to teach these clever foreigners something.

" Would you like a pair too, Madam?" she asked sweetly. "It can get very cold even at this time of year."

"Too! You mean you have bought a pair, Angus?" I replied.

"Aye, well, my blood must be getting thin, I'm thinking". he said, looking a wee bit sheepish. " I have neffer worn a pair of gloves in my life, but I admeet my hands were terrible cold in Thurso Bay thon time."

"None of us are getting any younger, Angus". I said, "Yes, I will buy a pair, please. Did you knit them yourself?"

"Yes, Ma'am. I knitted twenty pairs last winter. This winter I am going to start knitting jerseys. I am looking forward to that."

"Good for you." I said, "You keep one for me and I'll get it next year. Will you do that?"

"Yes, surely. I promised my granny the first one and you are taller. Can I measure you, please? What colour would you like" she asked. With that she produced a measuring tape.

"By gosh." I said as she measured the length of my arm. "You don't miss a trick. That's a very pretty colour you are wearing." It was an off white with lovat green and brown. "That same colour would be great. Can I feel it? Oh, that is very soft but strong. Do you live in Akureyri?"

"Yes, my father works at the whaling station. You would have passed it on your way in."

"We most certainly did." said I, holding my nose. "Does your father bring that smell home with him?"

"No. He does not. He changes his clothes and hosed down before he enters the house." she smiled, with a knowing look.

"It must be a terrible job. I hope it is worthwhile. What is your name so that I can contact you next year?" I asked thinking that I had talked myself into a contract.

"Margret. Would you not like a jersey too?" she said, turning to Angus.

"No. no. no. My niece in Eriskay sends me one every second winter, thank you very much. Anyway I don't think I will be back next year, I am getting too old for all this galavanting. But you look after yourself lassie" said Angus. With that he turned and started back to the boat.

"See you next year then", I said, as one of the younger crew members tried on one of her gloves, but I guess it wasn't just the gloves he was interested in!

Robert had suggested we meet at the new hotel for lunch. I was being shown to a table by the window of the weatherboard building, when I heard a familiar voice ordering a glass of wine at the next table. George Sim had his back to me.

"Do you mind if I join you George?" I said.

"Please do, Mrs Slimon." said George, rising to his feet and pulling out a chair. "Would you care for a bottle of beer, I was just ordering one myself? They don't serve wine"

"Yes, I will , thank you," I replied, "Robert should be any moment and he always enjoys a stout at this time of day. How did you get on with your wool discussion?"

" William agrees with me. Its a matter of 'its aye been' as you Scots say. The Danes have a very strong hold on the farmers and we have to organise something concrete to show that it would be advantageous to the farmers to sell direct to Bradford. I have given William a few contact names and I will have a word with them when I return. Ah, here comes the beer and your husband." said George, as he rose and pulled another chair to the table. The dining room was full and the smell of mutton stew wafted from the kitchen. "How was your morning, Mr Slimon?"

" Very interesting." said Robert as he poured himself a glass of beer. "I had a meeting with some of the farmers from Husavik which is in a sea-loch to the West. They have up to sixty miles to trek here with their horses and sheep, over difficult terrain. I suggested to them last year that they all get together and build a pier. This they did with great enthusiasm and they assure me we will be able to call on our next trip. Apparently, they have formed an association and they see all sorts of opportunities as a buying and selling group and also as a political voice when it comes to bargaining with the Althing."

"Althing?" queried George.

" Thank you," said Robert as the waitress placed a plate of what looked like tapioca porridge flavoured with vanilla in front of him. "Althing is the Icelandic parliament. In Shetland, Thingwall was the name of their Parliament in the days of the Vikings. The pier will mean, too, that their stock will be much fresher when we pick them up for what at the best of times is a wearing journey as you will experience on your return trip."

"Very good, Robert. Presumably you will be able to pay the farmers more for their sheep, as they wont have lost condition on the long trek". I put in.

"Thats right, Robina. All the sheep are paid by weight so everyone is a winner. They will get more and we will get more when we sell them at the market and there will be less death all round."

"So you could pick up their wool clip in Husavik as well" put in George and he went on to recount his mornings conversation with Mr Steffansson.

Plates of mutton stew with no vegetables but black bread were served. I noticed George trying to hide a disapproving look.

"I am glad you met Mr Steffanson, he is the man to get things moving." said Robert, "Its what these folk need. The price of wool is dropping so they require all the assistance they can get. With this new co-operative, they will be in a stronger bargaining position, thats for sure. Now I feel as if I need to stretch my legs. What about after coffee I show you this waterfall about a mile distant."

As there was demand for dining space, we were ushered through to a sitting room where we squeezed onto an old fashioned horse hair sofa, there not being enough chairs for everybody. The excellent coffee was served with a corn brandy and tea cake.

"I say, they know how to make coffee." said Mr Sim, "Tell me, Mr Slimon, I believe you are introducing money, or should I say gold and silver, to your trading. How does the system work when there are no banks or post offices here in Akureyri?"

" With difficulty," replied Robert. "Its only recently that a bank opened in Reykjavik, but hopefully there will be two or three more shortly, including here in Akureyri.

It is under the control of the Governor, there are no shareholders, just a manager, and one assistant who keeps the books. They have just started issuing Icelandic bank notes. The gold and silver can be exchanged for Icelandic currency. This, you might think, would be a problem, transferring gold to the capital safely, but in fact one of the attributes of the Icelander that has impressed me greatly is his honesty.

"Can you imagine even thinking to transfer gold without heavy guard across Yorkshire? That's admirable, especially considering their standard of living. Even so carrying gold across the country must be quite an onerous task. I believe you have a great man called John Coghill.

"Ah, yes,' said Robert, "But you haven't met John Coghill, a remarkable man. He is a son of the Caithness soil, but went to sea when his family moved to Orkney. When this Icelandic opportunity arose, I encouraged him to get his Masters Certificate, as he seemed ideally qualified to trade with the Icelanders as well. He is so respected by them now that he has become known as Horse Coghill or as they spell it Kogill, just as it is pronounced. It is entirely due to him that the trading has expanded in the way it has. A real character. There are a lot of stories about him but let me tell you them on our waterfall walk."

After passing a little Lutheran church, we were out into the country. Robert remarking that unless you had a job in Akureyri you were not allowed to build a house. But that policy was coming under pressure as with the expansion of the herring fishing, there were real problems during the season.

There was no clearly defined path and we had to navigate our way through little two foot high mounds. George was fascinated, as Robert explained that they were caused by frost and that the Icelanders regarded them as sacred. Something similar to our fairy mounds back home.

We could hear the waterfall before we could see it. But then familiar voices singing English songs were approaching from that direction. Round the side of the hill came Miss Speedie, Joan, Vaughan and their guides. They were all in high spirits. They had had their picnic and the sun had shone. Alex had been pleased with her obligatory sketch. Joan had really enjoyed her ride and was now confident of her four day trip to the interior. Vaughan had gone to the foot of the waterfall and had had a 'dook' and shower, which he had thoroughly enjoyed even though it was ice cold.

Soon we were standing on a hillock facing the waterfall. It was none too spectacular, but Robert had warned us not to expect too much. It was just a reason to stretch our legs. George said he would climb the hill and find his own way back, so after sitting for a few minutes enjoying the solitude we retraced our steps.

CHAPTER 5

REYKJAVIK TO THINGVELLIR

Having being brought up in Leith, I was more accustomed to going out in boats than riding horses and certainly not a four day marathon which the ride to Geyser and Gullfoss entailed. Miss Speedie and her party were wildly enthusiastic and one could not help being swept up in their enthusiasm of the adventure to come. But first we had a few hours to sample the delights of the Icelandic Capital, Reykjavik.

This is where all the foreign merchants stayed, mostly Danish and therefore a more European feel. The shops had a bigger variety of goods and the few hotels had larger menus with dishes to which we were more accustomed. For the first time we saw something resembling a road, although there was still no sign of wheeled transport.

We stopped to speak to a stone mason, who though Danish had learnt his trade in Scotland. He told us the Icelanders had believed it to be impossible to use lava as a building material. He was hoping to prove them wrong. What a boon that would be, as here was a material that was in abundance and of no other use.

Our first task was to make sure that everything was set up for our departure on the morrow. We were running on so tight a schedule that a departure on time was the first priority. The Icelanders never seem in a hurry and this is especially so where their horses are concerned. They seem to take for ever when saddling up. So patience is a key element on a trip such as we were about to encounter.

Robert had come along to see for himself how the organisation was going. A gentleman by the name of Zoega ran the business of hiring out the horses, baggage, tents and guides. He even provided special tents for we ladies which was a most welcome bonus. He and Robert had built up a good relationship and Zoega was known to be fair in his

Lake Thingvellatavn. The largest lake in Iceland, 25 miles in circumference.
Photo by the author

dealings. A few years ago Mt Hekla had erupted in March and Robert and Zoega had organised a party of thirty tourists, which required fifty horses for the fortnight excursion in July to the volcano. It had been the first major expedition in Iceland.

These trips had become an important part of Robert's business. Not so much as a financial venture, but more as a means for the Icelanders to promote their country. `He wanted to help put Iceland on the map as a tourist destination albeit an unusual one, with its volcanoes, glaciers, geysers and hot springs. New Zealand or America would be the alternative but they are months rather than days away.

All our bags had been assembled alongside the horses. They all had to be repacked into boxes and stowed in such a way that each pair were of equal weight to balance on these hardy little animals. Robert introduced me to Olafur, the leader of the expedition, who in turn introduced me to the two ponies delegated to me for the four day trip. I mounted one, a deep chocolate six year old that I was told was very patient and surefooted. We trotted round the enclosure without problem and,in fact, I found her more comfortable to ride than the bigger horses back home. I made a big fuss of her after dismounting and she seemed to know that there was something afoot, which I am sure she did as this was her fourth trip to Geyser. There were fifeen horses in all, two for each person plus three for the baggage.

We had an excellent guide book by one William George Lock, who had become a good friend of Robert. It was, perhaps, more for sportsmen but he had included the trip that we were undertaking. He made the point that tents were only used at Geyser as everywhere else one could find accommodation at farms and or parsonages. Geyser's eruption was unpredictable, therefore one should be as close at hand as possible.

Zoega then presented each of us with pairs of fisherman's waders and sou'westers, assuring us that these were essential for rivers that had to be crossed. We all tried them on for size which caused much laughter and merriment. At the same time Zoega collected the fee for the expedition. This amounted to twenty kroner per day or around £1. This covered the horses, the guide, food and accommodation as well as grazing for the horses.

We headed back to the town, where we had been invited by one of the merchants for dinner. It would be our last substantial meal for four days but as it was to be an early start on the morrow, I excused myself from the party. The Icelanders in true Scandinavian style insist on having toasts for every one and everything, so when Robert had replied to his, I felt it an appropriate time to excuse myself, so with good wishes ringing in my ears for the adventure to come I made my exit.

Although, Robert had been a good deal later to bed , he was as usual dressed and breakfasted before I appeared.

"It is a beautiful fresh morning. Ideal for your trip. I just wish I was coming. I hope Olafur has got every one organised. The first day is a long ride and that is why its best to get an early start. I hear that a student by the name of Magnus, wants to come just to improve his English as he hopes to go to University in Copenhagen, so you can be expected to have long intellectual conversations."

"Oh, I think I shall leave that to Miss Speedie and Co. They are far better educated than I." I protested.

"Not at all, there is no better accent than Edinburgh or should I say Leith and dare I suggest that you have much more knowledge of life and its problems than our southern friends."

Olafur had everything and everybody ready to go and what an exciting sight it made. The horses standing patiently, all saddled up, their loads all well balanced. Miss Speedie was in her usual high spirits and in no time she was mounted and encouraging us all to be on our way.

I am very partial to chocolate and thought it an appropriate name for my sturdy steed. I have no great affection for horses but these beasts seem different. Whilst living in the harshest of environments, one might expect them to be wild and of an independent nature. On the contrary they are friendly, extremely biddable and not surprisingly, surefooted.

And surefooted they had to be, for once out of Reykjavik, the path rapidly deteriorated into a boulder strewn plain and we depended on our horses finding their way. Olafur in the lead suddenly veered to the right on to higher ground and a stone free ridge, which was also firm and we fairly increased our pace. One was tempted to push the horses into a canter or even a gallop, but there was a long, long way to go and Olafur had warned us that he would not tolerate any nonsense.

Therefore, I don't think he was too amused when the worthy Captain of the *Camoens* came galloping up behind shouting and encouraging us to break into a gallop. I am not the most confident of horsewomen, so I was not tempted. Miss Speedie was indeed showing her competitive nature, but was persuaded to desist by brother Vaughan. So after riding with us for ten minutes or so, he wheeled round and with shouts of good wishes he sped off in high spirits.

Magnus, the student appeared by my side during this stretch of good ground and struck up conversation. His English was indeed excellent, but in querying me about life in Leith there were technical words that he had not heard before. 'Chandler' and 'marshalling yard' were among a few understandable ones that he had not come across. He had read many of our novels and had been thrilled to meet H. Rider Haggard who had been a passenger on the *Copeland* the previous year. Anthony Trollope had also visited Reykjavik on a yacht belonging to the renowned Lord Kelvin from Glasgow earlier that year and had found him an interesting character in that his political leanings were to the left, much akin to young Icelanders like himself but contrary to his fellow passengers, who were all very well to do.

One of the passengers he had struck up friendship with was Jemima Blackburn, who lived in an isolated spot on the West Coast of Scotland. Her talent as an artist had caused a stir with his fellow students. She had particularly wanted to draw bird-life, so he had volunteered to join the yacht on a picnic to a sea-loch north of Reykjavik, where he knew there was an abundance of sea-birds and where the gyr falcon nested. They had seen this magnificent bird and what had struck Magnus was her ability to recall in great detail the plumage and exact shades of colour throughout. The shape of beak, the length of claws and even the hawk-like intensity of the eye. Magnus had compared her drawing with that of others in the school library and he deemed Jemima's not only accurate but more life-like.

I was able to tell Magnus that Jemima was from a well known Edinburgh family, the Wedderburns, and although I had not met her, I had met some of her family at various Edinburgh functions. I added that he was indeed lucky to observe Jemima at work, as I had heard that even the great Edwin Landseer had said that he could teach Jemima nothing about her paintings of birds. I also knew that she had been to Iceland, in that George Lock, in writing his excellent Guide for travelers to Iceland, had referred to her when it came to women's clothing, as he himself had never travelled with women. She had travelled very light with just a Shetland shawl and light macintosh.

All the while we had been making good progress and Olafur called a halt for a break. The horses needed one more than we. They were soon grazing on a sweet patch of meadow-land whilst we untied the first of our picnic boxes. We had acquired some fresh fish before leaving Reykjavik and these were soon being cooked over a fire on skewers. It was a delicious meal and washed down with ice cool water from a little burn no distance away. Some of our own biscuits to finish off and we then took a short stroll to ease our limbs before we all saddled up again and were on our way.

I spent much of the afternoon alongside Vaughan who quizzed me at great length about Robert. He obviously had a great respect for his pioneering enterprise in establishing trade in Iceland. I emphasised how lucky Robert had been to find Captain John Coghill. Not only a good seaman but coming from respected farming stock he had struck a great rapport with the Icelandic farmers and he had won their respect by respecting them and always giving a fair price, contrary to the Danes who seem to have paid or bartered as little as possible . The Danes from whom he was taking trade tried to slur him by saying he was taking thier best stock and they would eventually suffer. To have done that would have been short term foolishness. Yes, he was taking the ponies when they were in their prime but he was careful to leave the best breeders. The Icelanders were no fools. They had not survived in this hostile environment for centuries without looking after their livestock in the most extreme conditions. Long severe winters along with all the disasters that erupting volcanoes and earthquakes could bring.

"What about the gold and silver?" asked Vaughan, "Surely that is what has given Robert the advantage."

"Yes, there is no doubt about that." I replied. "But that is the difference between Robert and the Danes. They just want to keep them under their heel while Robert sees great potential in this land for the people and wants to help them reach that potential. They have acquired a degree of independence, but without the gold they could not send their children to University or acquire decent fishing boats, and it has to be said, afford to emigrate. In past centuries these poor people would have died of starvation when they had experienced the severe winters like 1881 and 1882.

"My goodness, look at that" exclaimed Vaughan, pointing ahead and to the right. Suddenly the open dismal country that we had been passing through opened out even more and a vast lake stretched out to the horizon. It was like going from desert to fairyland. A cobalt blue expanse, which we were told was fed by glaciers thirty miles distant as well as hot springs deep below its surface.

"Thingvallavatn ahead" shouted an excited Miss Speedie. She had brought her horse to a halt and was soaking in the view from a rise a little off the track. "Isn't that just marvellous" she exclaimed. With that she dismounted and pulled out her sketching kit and in no time had pencilled in the features before us, which Magnus, self appointed guide, then described.

Lake Thingvellavatn is the second biggest in Iceland, about twenty five miles in circumference. Beyond are snow-peaked hills with steam coming from two geysers. In the foreground, is a great rupture of the earth where two walls run parallel. One being up to, perhaps, one hundred and eighty feet high, absolutely perpendicular. Apparently this is an important geological feature. The teutonic plates of America and Europe meet here but they are very slowly drifting apart. Beyond this a river leaps over the rocks above and roaring through boulders into the Execution pool. On the plain below it twists its way silently through the green pasture and into the lake, beside the church, parsonage and graveyard. The Execution pool, I should explain, was where women were thrust into a bag and thrown into drown for having committed the ultimate crime. Men, for committing similar crimes such as murder, rape or adultery were hanged.

We begin our descent down a rough path but not as dangerous as we were led to believe before we left Reykjavik. We make our way to the parsonage where we are to spend the night. The Parson is shortly expected, which is welcome news as he is reputed to be a great authority on all things Icelandic.

Embarrassingly, I and the other ladies have been given the best beds. Some have to sleep on the floor and after a ride of nearly forty miles, our weary bones are in need of a good rest. Our stomachs are also complaining and eventually after nine o' clock our meal arrives. It consists of coffee, brown bread, cheese, butter and boiled char. The fish newly caught from the Lake is excellent.

Before turning in we take a stroll through the graveyard and into the church, which like all the churches is rather plain. No stained glass but who needs that when one can be reminded of Gods magnificent creation by just looking through them. The view through this window is particularly magnificent with the shimmering lake and the hills dappled by the setting sun beyond. Here we meet the Priest Sira Paulsen, whose English is excellent and from him we learn how important the Church is in the countryside. As he goes round his flock, he not only instructs to their spiritual needs but also makes sure that the mothers are teaching their children to a good standard in the three 'Rs' and also Latin, Danish and even Hebrew. They also pass down the history and the great sagas of this island and, indeed, of the wider world

When a father comes to the Priest to ask him to officiate at the wedding of his daughter, the Priest has to satisfy himself that the bride has sufficient knowledge to pass on to her offspring. Likewise the groom, that he has the means to support a family, in the form of sheep, horses and cows or a fishing boat and tackle.

He shows us his Record of all his parishioners. From the very young to the elderly they are listed. What their progress has been over the previous twelve months, as well as a brief character sketch. Here truly is a shepherd of his flock. Not only nurturing with his Lord's teaching but helping to feed them with the knowledge of the world and to bring them up to be good citizens.

He counted himself extremely fortunate to be Priest in this historic place. The Althing is believed to be the oldest surviving parliament in the world, founded in AD 930. The first settlers wanted to get away from the rule of their royalty back home and thought they could set up their own laws and therefore a suitable site for a parliament would have to be found. Thingvellir was at a crossroads with a huge fish filled lake and ample firewood. The fact that the site had a stunning position was a bonus,according to the Priest because even the most tedious orator sounded dramatic. It took up to a fortnights travel for some from the northern parts to reach the Althing or parliament. It was not just the parliament, but a trading fair and entertainment and competitions of all kinds. There were long and often heated debates to make new or alter present laws. It is a pity that no one had ever drawn or painted a picture of the scene. It seems Icelanders, although gifted in poetry, music and literature, have never excelled in art. The Althing moved to Reykjavik less than one hundred years ago.

I was up early. I think disturbed by Miss Speedie, who was already down by the shore with Vaughan. He had found a fishing rod and was determined to catch fish for his breakfast. The Lake was like a mill-pond and this was the reason he gave for his lack of success. I wandered on and took off my socks and shoes where the rocks gave way to shingle and paddled along the shore splashing the ice-cold water over my face.

What a pity Robert wasn't here. He would have really enjoyed it. However, I was looking forward to our trip together with John Coghill up North when we would be buying sheep and horses and getting them loaded for the journey home.

I arrived back to the smell of fish sizzling in the frying pan.

"Aha, Mrs Slimon, you weren't out of sight two minutes and I had hooked a beauty." laughed Vaughan, "and then I caught three more in no time, so there is plenty for all."

Having fed well on the fish and a platter of cold meats and cheese and of course skyr, we were all in good form as we set off. The air was so clear and still as we bade our hosts farewell and with the view ahead of us, blue hills below the white of the glaciers we counted ourselves fortunate to have such good weather as there is nothing so miserable as being cold and wet on the back of horse.

CHAPTER 6

GULFOSS AND GEYSER

Olafur, I sensed, was not keen to have foreign ladies in his party but I think he was quietly surprised how well we had managed. Miss Speedie,in particular, was as competent as any man and was not slow in making everyone know it. Chocolate had seemed genuinely pleased to see me and I had made a big fuss of her before mounting.

The morning went quickly as we settled into our stride. Olafur insisted on being in front to keep a steady pace and negotiated over boggy ground and streams. We crossed a fairly wide river but it was shallow so we did not even have to dismount.

Thingvellir is roughly midway between Reykjavik and Geyser, but perhaps because we were now so confident and enjoying each other's company it seemed no time before we stopped for our midday snack beside a stream. Magnus had sped ahead and he had a fire going and was brewing up. Miss Speedie produced a tin of biscuits, on which we spread cheese. Tea always tastes better outside even tainted as it was with the wood smoke. There was a patch of scrub near-by from which Magnus had found enough dead wood to get the fire going. Vaughan had pulled some turf from the edge of a bank and added it to the blaze. Whilst the men smoked their pipes, we ladies stretched our legs in a hollow beside the burn. A shout from Olafur aroused us as the horses were beginning to wander away in search of a sweeter bite.

Soon we were on our way, this time on my reserve horse, which I had christened Cocoa, because that is what it sounded like, when Olafur pronounced his name. He was a light brown, so not at all unsuitable.

The country gradually got more fertile and we passed a number of farms. Some bigger than others. In these parts they seemed to have six to twenty cows and up to four hundred sheep.

I was quite content to ride along in silence and take in the splendid scenery. The gentle noise of the horses hooves and breathing as they panted up a slope with the occasional plaintiff call of a whimbrel added to the sense of desolation.

Midway through the afternoon a couple of natives heading in the opposite direction with a long string of horses, perhaps twelve or more, approached. Olafur stopped for a few minutes to exchange news. They were making for Reykjavik, and hoped to sell the horses to Scotland. Olafur pointed at me, indicating that it would be with Robert they hoped to make a deal. Olafur had a word with Magnus, who came back to say that they were father and son. The son was getting married and he needed money to buy some furniture for the room that his bride was to share with him

They had invited us to stay in his dwelling but unfortunately it was too far out of our way.

At last we saw spouts of steam in the distance indicating journeys end. A wind was getting up, which we began to ignore as our tents had to be pitched and there were no signs of shelter. However, the excitement grew as the 'stoker' appeared ever closer.

"Stoker?" queried Miss Speedie of Magnus.

"Yes" said Magnus "Stoker is smaller than Geyser but is much more reliable. In fact, performs every five or six minutes but is only half the height of Geyser. There is no telling when Geyser will perform and in fact you will be lucky to see him. Olafur tells me he has only seen it once and he is a regular visitor but it was a magnificent sight. It seems to be less frequent than in previous times. But one can always pray. We are proud of the fact that Geyser, which means gushing, is the term used throughout the world for all geysers."

"It is onomatopoeic." said Miss Speedie.

"That's a new word to me. What does it mean?" asked Magnus.

"Sorry, Magnus, your English is so good that I forget it is not your native tongue." said Miss Speedie. "It means the word is a description of the sound. In this case 'geyser'. Perhaps the best example is cuckoo being an exact description of the sound the bird makes."

"I'll take your word for it." replied Magnus. "We don't have cuckoos in Iceland. They live in trees, don't they and we are somewhat short of trees! I am getting the smell from the sulphur now."

Indeed we were and soon we were dismounting and while Olafur organized the horses, the menfolk started erecting the tents whilst the wind was not too strong. We made our way over to the geysers, which covered an area of perhaps three acres with lots of little pools bubbling away but dominated by Stoker and Geyser. This was what we had all come to see so we were determined to make the best of it.

There were three children, whom Magnus seemed to know, making their way towards us in a great state of excitement. It transpired they had succeeded in boiling three eggs. They had put them in a sock and suspended it into one of the pools.

"I am sure there must be ways one could make use of all that hot water in such a cold climate" said Mrs Joan.

"There are some very clever people working on that", said Magnus " I am sure one day we will be able to benefit from it."

"'Thar she blows" shouted Miss Speedie. I turned round just as the great spout reached its height and fell back to earth in a huge cloud of steam.

"Marvellous". exclaimed George. He had set up his camera and had obviously managed to snap the Stoker in full flow, by the way he was rubbing his hands together. George always rubbed his hands together when he was pleased whether it was after a good meal, making a telling point in a discussion or in this case, a personal achievement.

"I think", said George. "I had better put this camera away and go and help with the tents. That wind is certainly strengthening."

He need not have worried as the rest of the squad under the leadership of Vaughan and Olafur had all the tents erected and were beginning to cook the meal. Olafur had gathered some wood from a thicket a few miles back at a horse break. So he had a good fire going in a little hollow out of the wind. The smell of the wood smoke overpowered the sulphur and brought back memories of our courting, when Robert and I would go for picnics to Pathhead and pick brambles on Sunday afternoons.

Vaughan was now cooking some kind of mutton broth, cum stew. He was very secretive about what he had put in it but we were all so ravenous that we were not particularly worried. He passed round a bottle of whisky before tucking into this veritable feast and I poured a bottle of wine into our cups for the ladies.

To complete the repast, Magnus made some excellent coffee to go with cheese and biscuits and dark chocolate and we closed in around the fire which Olafur had stoked into a good blaze. In the gathering gloom Vaughan gave voice to some sea shanties and not to be outdone Magnus, who had a beautiful baritone voice, gave a rendition of what he said was an old Viking love song. This seemed a good opportunity to close proceedings as I was beginning to feel very drowsy and excuse myself thanking everybody for a lovely evening and wished them all good night.

Next morning the aroma of coffee brewing brought me very pleasantly to my senses. Getting dressed in the confines of a tent was made none more easy by limbs that were not used to seventy miles of rough riding. However, the effort was well worth while when I eventually pulled back the leaves of the tent to show the sun in a cloudless sky. The wind had dropped and the view to the south-east was fantastic. The snow capped peaks over the glaciers looked majestic. Magnus was identifying them all to Miss Alex and Vaughan.

"Magnificent, they may look" remarked Magnus. "but remember there are huge volcanoes lurking unseen below, that have wreaked devastation on this land for centuries past and we live in continual fear of when they may erupt. It is like a small country living next to a warrior nation never knowing when it might raid and burn your crops and destroy your homes. There is nothing you can do except thank God for every day you have in peace. And what a beautiful day this promises to be. That was a great mug of coffee Vaughan, almost up to Icelandic standard!

"Look, Olafur suggests he will stay with his boy to pack up our tents and equipment because we will be returning to here after viewing Gulfoss, which is two or three miles distant. The boy will stay here with fresh horses for us and Olafur will carry on towards Zog with the packhorses and we will catch him up."

It had been decided that with the fine weather and our good progress, we would have time to go to Gulfoss and see the waterfall. Olafur had been particularly surprised by us ladies and how well we had progressed. He kept muttering something which Magnus translated as "I do not believe it, I do not believe it." He was referring to our riding skills. The only other foreign ladies he had seen riding, rode side-saddle in the cumbersome chair-like saddle.

And so it was that Miss Joan, Miss Alex. Vaughan, George Sim, Magnus and I cantered off just after six o'clock. Two hours later, after making good time mostly in silence, we at first heard a distant roar and saw spray coming up from the ground. As we approached the noise increasing all the while, there appeared a canyon through which by far the largest volume of water that I had ever witnessed plunged from the plain above. ` An awe inspiring sight.

We stood on the lip mesmerised for many long moments taking in the sheer volume and force of the ice white cascade.

Then both Miss Alex and George, as if coming out of a trance, dismounted and set about finding the best location to sketch and photograph Gulfoss. There were different possibilities. Either from where we were standing looking upstream and above the gorge with the hills in the background and this is where Miss Alex chose to sit on a rock and taking out her pad and pencil began to draw. She had not taken her easel nor her artists box, as they were too bulky to carry on the small Icelandic horse . However, George was better equipped. Having travelled world-wide in many remote localities he had had a special rucksack made to carry his equipment. He now strode down a path leading to a rock half way down the waterfall. Setting up his telescopic tripod with the camera pointing towards the two hundred yards curtain of roaring water.

Meanwhile the rest of us climbed upstream until we were looking down on top of the fall and could see the gorge, perhaps four hundred feet deep, twisting through the landscape. It disappeared half a mile away round a corner but we could follow its path by the spray away into the distance.

Soon we were joined by George and Miss Speedie and whilst keeping a wary eye on our noble steeds lest they should wander too far, we enjoyed a snack of biscuits, cheese and apple. Magnus had collected a jug of water from the river and this was passed around. The coldness of it stung our tongues but most refreshing it was.

George remarked how within a short distance of four or five miles, we had witnessed water at boiling point and at freezing level. Where, he wondered, in the whole world could one have a similar experience.

"Well, if you don't know, George, I am sure none of us do." said Vaughan. "It must be a sight to see if the two extremes meet, as surely they must as there are so many hot springs and glaciers."

"There is one such place to the North of here in the next valley" interjected Magnus. "I have not seen it myself but I believe the women wash their clothes in the hot springs and then rinse them in the glacial stream five yards away. The children bathe in the mixture below where the water is warm. But, ladies and gentlemen, I think we should be moving. The day is going to be hot for the horses and we have a long trek in front of us."

Within ten minutes we were on our way and as the noise of Gulfoss slowly receded we were greatly satisfied that we had made the effort to go the extra mile as it were. We had in front of us a long day, which was to be made even longer by an unfortunate incident. Conscious of the long miles and a ferry crossing at the end of it, Olafur suggested we do a three hour stint instead of the usual two and give the horses an extra ten minutes rest. We were travelling through easy flat country and made good progress and reached a stream which made a suitable halt beyond that which Olafur had visualised. He suggested we have an hour and a half break as some of us were tempted by an inviting pool to give ourselves a good wash. It was a beautiful day and we all felt a bit sticky.

After our ablutions, with the women in one pool and the men downstream under a small waterfall, we were stretched out on the grass after our repast, well contented and not a little drousy. Suddenly Magnus gave a shout, firstly in Icelandic, then "The horses, the horses."

Having taken their fill of the lush grass around the stream they had started moving away and were half a mile distant already.

They had generally behaved so well that we had been lulled into a false sense of security. Magnus and Vaughan pulled on their boots and were racing away in pursuit. All we could do was wait patiently for their return. The horses were by now out of sight round a bluff. Poor Olafur was somewhat embarrassed. He said we should have kept to our well established routine, as now we had lost all the time and more that we had gained. It was another two hours before the horses returned, Vaughan explaining that his own horse was the culprit. He was a real character, named Apple, because of the apple shaped white patch on her black skin. When he caught sight of Vaughan and Magnus running behind them, he had taken off with the rest following. Magnus had climbed over a rise while the horses had followed the stream round a long bend. He thus got in front of them and the crisis was over.

For the rest of the day progress was slow. We were now in the heat of the day. It must have been eighty degrees, the hottest we had experienced and still many miles to go. We had another stop where the mood was somewhat subdued. For the first time Miss Alex was moody, but Vaughan, in spite of his midday excursion was still organising everybody with great good humour.

It was nearly three hours after midnight when we finally reached the banks of the river Zog. The ferryman's house was set back a quarter mile or so and when Olafur appeared with him five minutes after knocking on the door and shouting out his name, it could have been three o'clock in the afternoon, such was his good nature. It was about a mile to his ferry and we all trooped along behind.

The river was very fast flowing and twisted round rocks and plunged over small ledges. Apparently this was one of Icelands best trout rivers. Magnus said he had a friend who had caught fifty pounds of trout and char daily, during his weeks holiday. He also explained that Zog means the noise of drawing a long breath. The same noise that this tumultuous river made.

Whilst we unsaddled our horses in preparation for the crossing, the ferryman rowed out and hauled in his nets. We offered to purchase the few fine trout that he had in his nets. He was only too happy to oblige, keeping a couple for himself.

Magnus sat in the stern of the boat with all the saddles and gear at his feet and held on to the halter of his white horse, which in turn was tethered to half a dozen other horses. Magnus then had the task of keeping them together whilst the ferryman made another two trips. We bade our cheery conductor farewell with many thanks and prepared to make the last lap of our long day's journey.

Somewhere between four and five o'clock, when I am really feeling the need to lay down my weary head, the farmhouse of Villingavatn, where Olafur has booked us in, albeit at not so late an hour, suddenly appeared. After a few minutes the farmer emerged and bade us welcome.

He led us into the long narrow passage, that is common to Icelandic houses. Miss Speedie and I were ushered into the guest room, that has clearly just been vacated by women, who we now saw peeping round the doorposts. When Magnus and Vaughan squeeze past there are little giggles and whispers. George Sim, although somewhat older has an eye for the ladies and bid his hostesses a 'Good day' in his best Icelandic , which elicits more giggles as he is escorted into a dingy peat smelling room with the rest of the menfolk. Soon the elder ladies re-emerged with basins of warm milk for which we were most grateful as it was most refreshing.

The next thing I knew it is after ten o'clock and we are being hurried to partake of breakfast. But first let me describe our bedroom, which is typical of farmhouse guest-rooms. When I opened my eyes I found the eyes of Sira Halgrimur Petursson staring down at me with a disapproving air. He was one of the great poets of this country. Our two little beds are placed along one wall and the rest of the furniture consists of a table, a chair, an American clock and a somewhat tarnished mirror. There is one small window constructed not to open. So the room is decidedly airless. No doubt this is the lesser evil when it comes to winter where the priority must be to keep the house warm.

On the beds are feather mattresses and instead of blankets the Icelanders use quilts filled with eiderdown. It is, quite rightly highly esteemed, for it is wonderfully warm and comfortable, so much so that I had great difficulty in pulling my complaining limbs out of its warm softness.

Breakfast was served in our room with the eyes of Mr Petursson upon me as I tucked into the fresh trout purchased earlier that morning, hot milk, skyr, kaka or cake, rugbrand or rye bread and skonrug, a rusk. The rye bread was very thick and black but the rusk is very palatable. We top up with some of our own tinned meat, white bread and cocoa.

On going outside we found Magnus speaking to the farmer. Apparently, the farm was above average in terms of acreage or as he corrected me, square miles. A small farm supports perhaps two cows and fifty sheep whilst a large one twenty cows and perhaps, five or six hundred sheep. He grew a little potatoes and turnips but the farm was mostly under grass. The great challenge was to secure as much hay as possible during the summer months.

"Magnus, ask him who is the richest man in Iceland." Vaughan says.

"The Bishop" comes the reply. A man is considered rich if he

Picnic at Gulfoss 1885. Used by permission of the Akureyri Folk Museum.

possesses 10,000 kroner and very rich if he has ten times that amount. Vaughan quickly calculates that our ministers earn roughly ten times that amount.

I ask Magnus about Sira Halgrimur Petursson. The reply comes back that he is one of the great Icelandic authors and then goes on to list poets, playwrights and other great authors.

"If you have playwrights, have you got any theatres?" I ask.

"No," says Magnus "but on occasion a stage is erected in Reykjavik and these have proved popular."

By midday we are on our way and a very rough way it is. The poor horses having to pick their way through a lava bed with some very steep rises and descents. Today, I have started on Cocoa as she seemed to be the fresher after yesterday's long day and with the escapade in the middle. After a couple of hours we halt on a small rise and admire the view from where we have come with a last look at Lake Thingvellavatn shimmering in the distance. Magnus points out Thingvellir, just visible with the islands of the Lake standing out against the snow capped mountains in the distance. In the foreground between the ugly lava strewn boulders, clouds of sulphur emanate everywhere.

Soon we are able to make good progress when we descended onto a grassy plain. I was expecting to see sheep or horses grazing but not a beast is there to be seen. On querying Magnus, he can give no explanation at all. At last we can see the distant ocean and stop for our meal, but do not tarry as there are still several miles to go.

It was nearly ten o'clock when we mounted a small rise and the ocean was set out before us and at last signs of human life in the form of strings of horses being led towards the port. Both men and women led the horses, some of the women sat astride but most sat in a peculiar chair shaped construction, which can best be described as armchairs, similar to our barstools. When walking the women covered up their heads with shawls and when on horseback they used multi-coloured scarves crossed at the front.

At last we entered the town and are soon passing the Island Hotel, where some familiar faces emerged to welcome us back. Soon after heartwarming thanks to Olafur, we are joining our friends. Never did a long cool drink go down so well.

CHAPTER 7

HONOURED BY THE MERCHANTS

Last year Robert had been honoured by being given a reception by the Icelandic Government. It was a grand occasion at which the government recognised the benefit to Iceland of trade being opened up between our two countries and also the way Robert and John Coghill had treated the people in a fair and generous manner. This year the Icelandic merchants, who it has to be said, did not always see eye to eye with the administration, decided to show their gratitude by holding a party of their own. Robert wanted it to be as informal as possible and so as not to tread on any toes had suggested they come on board the *Camoens*.

I had a hurried bath in the hotel, and could have easily soaked for another half hour to ease away the aches and stiffness of the last four days in the saddle but Robert gets nervous about making speeches, especially to foreigners who might misinterpret, albeit unintentionally, what he had to say. His other fear was that he might be persuaded to take too much alcohol during the meal before he made his speech and that if I was at his side, he hoped I might have a deterring effect on his hosts. I, myself, was a wee bit nervous of the Danish merchants, as like all Scandinavians, they can be very persuasive where alcohol is concerned and having not had a decent nights sleep for some time, I thought it best to keep to water.

The Merchants wives and servants had taken over the Galley for the day and our ship's cook had spent the morning with them explaining the intricacies of on board catering. Leslie hailed from Peterhead and had an accent to match. Apparently Angus had to be called in as translator and there was much hilarity all round. Leslie had started life on the fishing boats but he had managed to break a leg on his third trip out and on returning to duty had been confined to the galley, which he had found very frustrating, whilst his mates were doing the real work. He had gone back to work before the fracture had healed properly and as the North Sea is not the kindest environment for broken legs, the result was a permanent limp. However, he found that he enjoyed cooking and indeed had a real flair for concocting exciting dishes from the few ingredients that could be stowed on board.

I had packed one of my special dresses for the occasion, while Robert had got a kilt especially made. Many of his Icelandic friends seemed to be fascinated by the wearing of the kilt and would ask him why neither he nor any of the crew wore one. In spite of his trying to explain the Highland history of the kilt and its being banned a hundred years ago, they were not satisfied, so we had thought it might go down well on this celebration of fifteen years of a relationship with Iceland. Getting dressed in the confines of the cabin took all of our somewhat limited patience, but I was ready as I heard the first of the Merchants arriving. It seemed a bit strange to be a guest in ones own vessel and they, I think, felt a bit odd too.

I had already met some of our guests, but not their wives who all came in their traditional dress. Unfortunately not many of them have very good English. I was placed next to Robert and a Mrs Jonsson. She is the wife of the Merchant, who has organised the evening and a nephew of Sugersson, the Liberator of Iceland.

There are twelve merchants, nine of whom have wives or partners plus, Captain Robertson, Robert, myself and John Coghill, who burst in just as one of the merchants, whose father is a minister, is about to say grace. A great cheer of welcome goes up as John circles the table greeting everyone in true Scandinavian style. With many apologies he takes his seat beside Mrs Jonsson, a very attractive lady, who greets him like a long lost son. He explains in his broad Caithness accent, that his lateness was due to a late consignment of horses. The farmer had proved hard to deal with and John had by way of compensating him for what the farmer thought a poor offer, had taken him for a drink in the Island Hotel.

"He were a drouthy chiel" John concludes. By his general demeanour, I conclude that John too was pretty drouthy.

I have referred to John once or twice so far, but here allow me to describe him and his character. He always wore a Glengarry above his full black bushy beard. Being big framed he gave the appearance of an Icelandic hero of old.

A man of tremendous energy he had to cover vast distances in a short time and would ride non-stop till nightfall only stopping to change horses of which he always had many. Such was his reputation that there was a saying "ride like Kogill".

He was renowned for his absolute fairness in dealing, to the extent that he would pay more to someone who was not asking enough. But woe betide anyone who tried to cheat John. He would simply not deal with him again. He was an expert on ageing a horse by its teeth and could judge the weight of a sheep by feeling its back and tail.

His Icelandic was limited but seemed to have a good grasp of all the swear words which he used liberally, though I have to say never in front of me. But, of course, this all added to his attraction to teenage boys, who regarded him as a hero.

He had a small house attached to the Island hotel in Reykjavik where he frequented the bar and teased the young ladies and laughed loudly when they rejected his advances. He had a reputation for being a ladies man and indeed had several relationships throughout Iceland.

As with buying sheep from the less well off, he was generous to the poor of the country trying to encourage them to be more self-sufficient. Annually he would give them packets of turnip seed.

Mr Johnsson had been most impressed by John's concern at the danger of disease and his letters to the parliament advising them to recruit veterinary surgeons. If disease took hold it could decimate the export of sheep.

Mr Johnsson then asked everyone to stand and he led the Icelanders in a rousing rendition of their National Anthem to the tune of 'God save the Queen', which, after we were seated, he proudly translated as the following;

Fair Iceland, old as fire, – beloved native land
Mountain bride our hearts desire
Sweet fosterland.
While woman loved shall be
By man; or sun shines free;

Captain John Coghill. He always wore his Glengarry. Photo with permission from John C. Blind. **Inset photo:** Weydale Mains, Thurso where John Coghill was born. Notes the Caithness slab wall front of the house. Photo by the author.

Icelandic flag made by the Merchants wives for Robert Slimon in 1884. Presented to the Iceland 'National Museum by the author.

While land is girt by sea

Thou shalt be dear.

He also claimed that the tune had been originally composed in Iceland. I did not like to dispute the point, but made a mental note to check our newly acquired Encyclopedia Brittanica.

The meal was truly excellent being interspersed regularly with toasts, The *Camoens*, Scotland, Scottish and English merchants and traders, the Icelandic horse and all livestock, the fish in the sea. Each trader in turn rising, first filled the glasses and then in surprisingly good English delivered their toast.

We started with platters of fish, both river salmon and trout and sea cod, halibut, whiting and herring. This was followed by huge dishes of meats, beef, mutton, reindeer and ptarmigan. Potatoes and turnips with a thick gravy completed the course.

I was encouraging Robert to eat as much as possible to soak up the copious amounts of alcohol that seemed to be coming round in a continuous stream. Meanwhile, on my other side Mr Johnsson was getting evermore loquacious. He became more and more vindictive about the Danes, inferring that they treated the Icelanders as second or third rate citizens. If they were in a hotel or boat, they ignored the local people and would push past them in a shop or on the street. Again I did not dispute his assertions, no doubt there was an element of truth in it, but individually the Danes were very pleasant. But were Britons any better? The stories coming back from various parts of the globe, were not to be proud of. We tended to treat many of the peoples of the world as savages. Is it not natural for nationalities to draw together when in company, especially when there is a language problem? Did we not tend to ignore the Icelanders on our trip out? I did make an effort to include them at meal times, but they seemed to prefer their own company, which is quite understandable.

Rhubarb and a skyr custard and lashings of cream was followed by excellent coffee during which Mr Johnsson rose to his feet to give the main toast of the evening.

This was to Robert and Captain John Coghill. He recounted how the Icelanders had first been wary of 'Horse Kogill' as he came to be known. They had only ever been used to the Danes and here was a foreigner speaking what he claimed to be English, but even his fellow countrymen had difficulty understanding his Caithness accent. However they were soon won over by his stocksmanship and his good but fair prices. The offer of gold rather than barter or the Danish Krona had been another great influence. This action had done more for the Icelandic economy than any other. A number of farmers children were now able to go to University. Farmers were able to buy or build fishing vessels to compete with foreigners. Generally there was a greater feeling of confidence and independence. In fact, this was partly to the detriment of the Merchants as it gave the farmers extra bargaining power. He explained, too, how Robert had helped the farmers in time of bad weather by hauling hay to the North to help keep the stock through the winter, whereas the Danes would take the fattest beasts and offer poor prices or cheap goods in exchange. How he had encouraged them, nay bullied them into building piers for his ships.

He rounded off his speech with a few of Kogill's more eventful exploits both as sailor and stocksman which brought much laughter. He then called on the ladies to make a presentation. Both Robert and John were obviously very touched as they presented firstly, the Icelandic flag of Independence to each in turn. A white gyr falcon on a blue background, both finely sewn by the merchants wives and then for the boat, a portrait of Sugersson the Liberator of Iceland and uncle of my dinner companion. This was indeed a great honour, as Mr Johnsson said, Iceland did not have Knighthoods or Orders of the Bath or Thistle or even Gyr Falcon but he hoped that we would see it as their equivalent.

Robert started his reply by doing a twirl of his kilt , which was much appreciated and a few suggestions as to what might be worn underneath. This seemed to go down particularly well with the ladies!

He related how he had first started his trade importing ponies or horses from Germany. Although a ship chandler, he like John had been brought up on a farm. People thought him foolhardy, if not cruel, to contemplate sailing through the Pentland Firth and Northern Atlantic with livestock aboard. They did not know how hardy the Icelandic stock was. Cheers. They did not know Captain John Coghill. Cheers. Here he paid tribute to John's undoubted seamanship, a skill that , perhaps the Icelanders did not fully appreciate as they mainly knew him as a trader. It was his suggestion to put nine inches of sand on the decks to prevent the beasts from losing their footing in stormy seas. But we had been fortunate with all the sea Captains, none more so than Captain Willie Robertson. More cheers. His seamanship was second to none and as a mine host, which a passenger vessel, also entails, many travellers had told him that his concern for their well-being and comfort was only out-done by his concern for the animals that he was transporting. Robert went on to relate some of the escapades on both land and sea. Some hair-raising, others hilarious. He concluded by saying that he thought that Iceland was on the threshold of greatness, with potential for increased markets for agricultural products and fish. A nation that had survived isolation, Arctic weather, earthquakes and volcanoes could only get stronger with the better communications and developments of the modern world and he wished them well.

John Coghill concluded a most enjoyable evening by first stating that as nobody understood him anyway he would keep his speech short and ended by thanking the Merchants, or more particularly their wives, in his own peculiar brand of Icelandic.

CHAPTER 8

BORDEYRI, EMIGRATION AND EXPORT

We sailed with the tide at twenty minutes to six the next morning. I did not hear Robert go above, so soundly did I sleep. The pitching of the ship brought me too, but I am afraid I rolled over and watched the seas heaving outside the port hole. We were to berth in Bordeyri next morning, so it would be a day of catching up with all the happenings, whilst we were on our trek.

When Robert came in, I had dosed off again.

"You really should not miss this part of the trip. The scenery is spectacular and there is a lot of activity on the ocean as well."

After last nights feast, I needed only a light breakfast. Captain Robertson was about to descend to the saloon as I came on deck.

" Good morning Mrs Slimon. Be careful, she is slewing a bit. The wind and tide are at right angles to each other so be careful. That was a wonderful evening last night was it not?"

"Indeed it was Captain." I replied. "I am not sure that I have quite recovered yet. Tell me who do all these fishing boats belong to?" There were boats to port as far as the eye could see.

"Ah, they are all French. They reckon there ten thousand Frenchmen out there. There is a great demand to join their navy. So the government encourage them to go to the Arctic on fishing boats to sort out the men from the boys. Many of them think the navy is a tour round the ports of the Mediterranean. Gutting fish for up to sixteen hours a day in freezing sleet changes the outlooks of a few. The fish are salted into the holds in the centre of the vessel."

"Morning, Mrs Slimon" John Coghill and Robert appeared behind me as the *Camoens* gave a lurch throwing me into Capt. Robertson's arms.

"Now, I told you to be careful, the deck is very slippy", said he. "If you will excuse me, I must have a word with Angus."

"How is he doing, Captain?" asked Robert.

"Extremely well considering. But he tends to forget this and that. He should have sent tea and a piece up to the bridge half an hour ago." said the Captain. "It is just his age, but we could not have managed without the old devil." With that he disappeared below.

"I'm getting that way masel'. said John. "I used to able tae mind the number an' price of all the sheep an' horses from all the fermers whae I bought from the year afore without lookin' at me notebook. Nae longer, I doot.

"From what I heard last night , John, the farmers are all looking forward to your visit." I said. "They had a good lambing and they have had a good summer so the lambs will be in good condition."

"Aye, that'll be right enough an they'll be expecting more money but it has been a good year at home too, so there'll be a glut on ae market." replied John.

"It's always a problem to know how much money to bring to Iceland" said Robert. " I hate being caught out by bringing too little, but we can lose a lot of interest by bringing too much and going back home with it. How is Angus today, then?"

Angus was ascending the gangway with a box and pail. "Ach, no very well at all, at all. Did I not forget to put up the tea. Ach, so they'll not be too well pleased up there, I am theenking."

"Let me carry that, Angus" said Robert, . "There is a big swell on."

"Naw, naw, sir." replied Angus. "My mind might be getting doddery, but my legs are still fine. Anyway, is it not myself that will have to be apologising to them myself?"

"Poor Angus," said John, taking out his pipe "When I get to that age I'll have my feet up by the fireside."

"And where will that fire-side be, John, Edinburgh or Iceland?" asked Robert,knowing full well that John, whilst having a wife in Edinburgh, had also a few ladies in Iceland with whom he had children to and from all accounts would happily have him as a permanent lodger.

" I don't really know, to tell ee the truth." said John, lighting another match whilst shielding the bowl from the wind. "My wife does not know anywhere else but Edinburgh, but I would like to try Orkney where the family moved to when I left home. I would like to get a wee placey and buy some Icelandic sheep and horses and a couple of their kye. They are awfie good doers. Plenty creamy milk and hardy."

"Olafur told me that they are the most efficient converters of grass into milk of any breed," I interjected. "They had compared them with all the other British and European breeds. But I don't suppose that is too much of a surprise, considering that to even survive up here and rear a calf is a miracle in itself. It all adds to Charles Darwin's theory of the survival of the fittest. But tell me, John, are there any big herds. I have only seen farms with two or three. Enough for their own needs."

" Sooth of Reykjavik there are bigger herds that make cheese an' butter and as ae toon grows, so will ae demand." replied John. "'eir climate is not that different from Orkney and I think 'ere is great potential for ae improvement of grassland. 'ey have an abundance of potash from ae volcanoes, but 'ey need phosphate and lime and of course, ae cost o' transport is very high, as we know."

Whilst John was speaking George Sim had joined us and said. "What has struck me, is not only the lack of cultivation, but the lack of implements. You said the climate compares with Orkney, I find myself comparing it to the South Island of New Zealand. There they are fairly improving the land and have ploughs and other cultivating machinery that we have in England. But perhaps that is the difference. The Britons that have gone out have taken their machinery with them and know how to use it, whereas here they would have to be trained, as indeed would their horses."[1]

"But, for all that, they depend on the sea for their wealth, on the fishing and that is where the great potential lies," commented Robert. "When they get that under their own control this could be a wealthy nation. Europe is becoming a hungry continent. However back to the present. Do you know how many emigrants are to be picked up in Bordeyri, John?"

" No, I don't." replied John. "Originally there were supposed to

---

[1]   Appendix 4 Exports

be eighty or so, but because of the good spring and summer, some of them now are determined to hang on for another year. They will have plenty hay and they should get more money for their sheep. Most who sold horses were well pleased with the condition they were in. So was I for that matter. I hate not being able to buy them when they are not fit enough for the journey. "

" It must be heart wrenching to have to make the decision." I said. "Leaving family and friends behind, knowing that you will never see them again. It is such a long journey too. Did you not have an awful experience when the *Camoens* was damaged up North and the poor emigrants were left for weeks in Bordeyri with little food?"

"That is right," said John. "In fact, the ice closed in and she had to hug the coast to get out. I heard 'ey were still in Borderyi and managed to get there eventually, hoping that they had gone home. But of course 'ey had sold everything to pay for their passage. 'ey were in a terrible state. I knew that the *Miaca*, our new wee boatey was in Reykjavik, so I rode as I had never ridden before and got it up here. We managed and 'ey were clothed in Reykjavik a few days later but there were a few deaths, including children before 'ey reached Winnipeg. But the young ones have heard about this wonderful country where crops grow so easily an' ae climate is better. 'Ey know that they are never going to go to bed hungry again. Some of them ask me what would I do if I were them. I think back to my own youth knowing that ae farm could not support all of our family, but I had always wanted to go to sea, so it was quite an easy decision to make. But I would fine like to be able to go back to ae land now. Ae difference with them is that 'ey know 'ey will never see Iceland again. I have travelled the world and I think 'ey are more attached to 'eir own country than any other I can think of. I think what 'ey don't realise that in places like Winnipeg 'ey wont see the sea again either. Its not till you are away from ae sea for a whiley that you realize you can't live happily without it."

"Mind you it is not just starvation that it is taking them away." said Robert. "There is always the ever-present fear of earthquakes and volcanoes. These sort of catastrophes can be absolutely devastating, not just at the time but for years afterwards. Imagine if Arthur's Seat were still active, there would be no Edinburgh today. Mind you speaking as a Leither that would be no bad thing! Seriously though, many see emigration as an opportunity to better themselves . Be it as joiner, banker or shop-keeper, or indeed farmer. To raise a young family in Canada today would be wonderfully exciting. There is I am sure huge potential in forestry and mining as well as agriculture."

At this point Miss Whyte came on deck with Vaughan. " Good morning, Miss Joan, Vaughan. Enjoy the scenery. It is well worth a painting" said Robert.

"With this swell, I think I will just attempt a sketch of these fantastic cliffs and do the paint work when we are in port" said Miss Joan. "I have had too many botches. Anyway, I would like to put in some gannets, both flying and diving. They are really fantastic. I have really got into birds. Magnus showed me some of Jemima Blackburn's bird paintings. They are absolutely amazing."

"I could arrange to take you onto the Bass Rock in the Firth of Forth" I said. I knew the head light-keepers wife and had arranged a trip when her husband was starting his spell of duty there a few years ago. "There are more gannets there than practically anywhere. You can walk amongst them when they are nesting. It is an amazing experience."

"I have sailed round it often, but never landed, of course." said Vaughan. " But that would be wonderful, Mrs Slimon. Next spring, Joan, you come north and I will show you the sights and we could pick a calm day to land on the Bass."

"Oh, I would love that, Vaughan." Miss Joan whispered. She was clearly bowled over by Vaughan, who was very gallant and had helped her to gain confidence on the trek, which had been a completely new experience for her.

" Are these not just beautiful boats?" said Vaughan, pointing. A small open decked fishing boat with two men on the oars slipped by on the starboard beam.

" Aye, 'ey poor Icelanders. That's all 'ey so and so Danes will let them fish in, or did" said John. "There are a few now with bigger boats, but you're right Vaughan, they're beautifully made."

"Very similar to the Shetland boats and all descended from the Viking longships, I believe." said Robert. '" Oh, here comes the sun, I think we are going to have another good day."

"Indeed we are." said Vaughan. "Look at the light on these cliffs, George. Does that not cry out for a photograph? I am away to get my gear. Are you coming to get your easel, Joan?"

" No, I don't think so, I prefer terra firma for painting," replied Joan. "Perhaps you could explain the art of photography to me. I quite fancy the idea of getting a camera."

I am not sure how true that statement was. I think Joan was beginning to prefer Vaughan's company to Miss Speedie's, whose paintings were excellent but she tended to let everyone know it, which must have been a little dispiriting for Joan.

After they had gone below, followed by George, who also declared he would get his camera, I turned to Robert. "How's poor Ewan? I think I should go and have a word with him."

"He's been great this last day or two, but we have seen this before and then he has a relapse. But yes, go and have a word and see what you think. Vaughan has been very attentive, going in morning and night and spending time with him. When I thanked him, Vaughan said that he found him a most interesting case and was planning writing a case study on him when he returned to Edinburgh, although it isn't his line of medicine. I think it is Jim who is looking after him today. He seems to have struck up a bond with him and they play endless games together"

I made my way forr'ard to the little cabin and knocked on the door. "Come in, come in, come in," a cheery voice said. "Hullo, hullo, hullo and how are you today, Mrs Slimon? I am extremely well myself. The weather is fine, Jim is fine, so I am sure you must be fine too. In fact, we are both so fine that we would like to sing you a little song." All this gushed out of Ewan without hardly a breath.

With that he stood up, hauling Jim with him and went into a rendition of "Bonnie Bobby Shaftoe," dancing a hornpipe at the same time.

"What a beautiful dancer you are." I said "And, I may say singer too. I really mean it."

"Not much room in here, Mrs Slimon. I am sure Mr Slimon would not mind if we went up on deck." said Jim. Now I am thinking, is this a ploy just for some fresh air. Well, I thought Robert said he had been better and there were plenty of hands around if he should show signs of jumping overboard. I looked at Jim, who gave a slight nod. He was a sensible lad and knew Ewan better than anyone.

"OK" I said, "I am sure you will cheer the passengers up a bit."

The look of pleasure that came over his face, was that of a wee boy being given some sweets.

Ewan very politely asked me to lead the way and with Jim coming behind, we emerged on deck. I thought to draw attention to Ewan by making a small introduction but he was already dancing across the deck doing cartwheels and somersaults. He then, standing to his full height, drew in a big breath of air. Living in his cramped space, the atmosphere was pretty stale. He next performed an excellently executed hornpipe, humming loudly all the time. I attended dancing classes in my youth and I am sure my teacher would have been well pleased with how he pointed his toes. He finished with a final flourish leaping in the air and then executed a low bow. We all stood and clapped and cheered loudly to Ewan's obvious pleasure and embarrassment. At a loss what to do next we persuaded him to rest.

Vaughan disappeared and returned with his violin. He proceeded to play the 'Blue Danube'. George Sim, who seemed to enjoy any kind of ceilidh, asked me to dance. Miss Speedie grabbed, a rather taken aback, John Coghill and Robert asked Miss Joan. All the time, Ewan waltzed by himself. The sea was now almost a flat calm and with the sun on the snow capped hills it was one of these memorable moments, all thanks to poor Ewan. When we had finished Vaughan started to play a jig. Again Ewan was on his feet and with amazing footwork, got us all clapping. Faster and faster Vaughan played but he could not exhaust young Ewan. Eventually to more applause the jig ended with Ewan and Vaughan locked in a warm embrace of mutual admiration.

Robert sent down for mugs of tea and sandwiches, and although Ewan was shouting for more dancing, he eventually tucked into 'a muckle meat piece' with great gusto.

I got into conversation with George who was expressing the opinion that he was disappointed with the lack of cultivation around the Icelandic lochs or fjords and what potential there was. Suddenly there was loud snoring and turning round poor Ewan was lying full length on his bench. Apparently his sleep pattern was very irregular, which was very tiring for Jim and other members of the crew who were detailed to spend time with him.

The evening turned into a good ceilidh with songs, recitations, Vaughan on the violin and plenty story telling. Robert and I strolled on deck as we watched the setting sun just before midnight. We were very near the Arctic circle and once again we were blessed with a beautiful sunset.

"We are as near to Greenland as we'll ever be. That's the tip of the Snaefellsnes peninsula." said Robert pointing behind us. "I believe if you climb to the top of that glacier, Snaefellsjokull, which is higher than Ben Nevis you can see Greenland to the North West on a good day."

George was taking a photograph of the sunset from the port side. "Do you know why it is called Greenland, Mr Slimon?" he asked.

"It is an interesting story, George. One that is rapped up in the old Icelandic Sagas. About a hundred years after Iceland was settled, the people were finding the conditions too harsh and one Eirik the Red got embroiled with a richer neighbour, which ended in bloodshed. The Icelanders were desperately trying to be a peaceful nation and so Eirik was banished from the country for three years. Rather than returning to South West Norway from where he had come, he decided to sail West along the 65th parallel to lands that were rumoured to exist. Thus he reached Greenland but avoided the east coast where a previous storm had landed his countrymen where they nearly all starved to death. Eirik sailed round Cape Farewell and found a beautiful green area in which to rear his stock. The climate then was warmer than it is today. With an abundance of fish as well as the ivory of the narwhal, seal skins and the fur of the polar bear to sell to the European markets, he saw great opportunity for settlement."

"After his three years were up, Eirik the Red returned to Iceland and had no difficulty in persuading enough people to travel back with him and create a settlement. This was helped by his reference to this new land as Greenland. As was tradition he would have authority as the First Settler. So in the year around 986, I think, twenty five ships with three hundred emigrants aboard set sail. They took cattle and sheep and everything to prepare a settlement. But only fourteen ships made it. Apparently they encountered a freak storm, possibly caused by an undersea earthquake."

"Then Eirik's son, Leif, had gone back to Norway and had been converted to Christianity by King Olaf. He set sail back to Greenland. He hit bad weather and fog and twice landed on land that was comparatively flat and wooded. He knew that this could not be Greenland and sailed on. Eventually at the fourth attempt they saw steep mountains and glaciers. They then worked out where Eirik's place must be. So it was that America was first discovered. In fact, there are mentions of other Viking landings long before Columbus set sail."

'"So the Vikings found America and they lost it again! Very careless of them! " said George. "Tell me, were there Eskimos not living in Greenland at that time or Iceland for that matter?"

"They were in Greenland, but I don't think there has ever been any traces found in Iceland." replied Robert. "Come on, I think it is time we turned in, it is getting rather chilly."

We breakfasted sailing into Bordeyri on another sparkling morning. Robert reported that it was very cold on deck, but the sun was in a cloudless sky and by the time we emerged it was pleasantly warm with Bordeyri fast approaching. The stewards were getting the accommodation for the new passengers ready.

"I think I will go and see Captain Robertson," said Robert. "I know he is nervous about the approach to Bordeyri, as there are shallows that have to be negotiated. It is well that the sea is flat calm."

"I thought he was not his usual cheery self this morning," I said. " I am sure you have every confidence in him."

"I do, I do." he replied, "But these sand banks can shift about from year to year. We found that up near Akureyri." With that he bounded up the gangway.

The *Camoens* was now slowly weaving her way towards what was no more than a collection of houses. It would be an exaggeration to call it a village let alone a town. As we approached people began to emerge from a big shed that apparently served as a warehouse. These were obviously our passengers.

We were all leaning on the rail looking down on these poor folk.

"What a dispirited looking lot" said Miss Speedie. " You would think they would be excited about coming aboard a big ship."

" I would think you would be dispirited if you were leaving your homeland forever." retorted Miss Joan. "What do you say, Vaughan?"

"Yes, I think it must be terrible for the old folk especially." said Vaughan "but some of the youngsters are desperate to get to this land of milk and honey in Western Canada. John tells me that these are very poor folk, most of whose sheep and cattle starved to death through the winter. John is worried in that he thinks two of the young women are pregnant. It is a long, long journey that they face. They will have very little money to pay for food, let alone decent clothes to keep them warm on the six week journey and a Canadian winter ahead of them."

"Its a very difficult problem." I said. " The thing is we are only contracted to provide them with hot and cold water. They provide their own food to take them to Granton and Glasgow. Some of our trips we have had over seven hundred. They seem to usually have plenty dried fish, smoked meat, whey and cheese, with that black bread that we had at Thingvalla."

"I was thinking about what you said, Mrs Slimon." said George. " If you are taking seven hundred at a time, is the population not at risk of becoming too small? Will there be enough left to look after the beasts and teach the children? Presumably whole families will go and then their farm will be abandoned and what about the stock?

"You are quite right. There is a worry that some parts of the country are just going to be abandoned. But the fact is, the recent winters that they have had to endure have led to deaths due to starvation. The stock too have suffered badly. It is hard to know if this is the start of another ice age or just a series of cold winters. Certainly this summer has been excellent so perhaps it will be warmer again. The ironic thing is that I feel partly responsible, in that because they now have money, they are able to pay for their passage,"

"Oh, look at these two wee children," said Miss Joan pointing at two faces peeping out of their mother's skirts.

I have to say I was not very happy, as they were to simply lie on the deck or in the hold should the weather be rough. They were, as Vaughan said, all ages with families with babies and grandparents The Icelanders wanted it to be as cheap as possible as they simply had very little money and this was but a short hop on their long journey to Western Canada. Robert had contacts in Reykjavik and Akureyri where clothes and bedding were provided by some of the better off people. We would be calling in at Akureyri, so hopefully we would get supplies there, for indeed some of the folk seemed to be clothed in nothing but rags. Their worldly belongings were tied up in bags. Some of them had already been in Bordeyri for two or three days. It was up to two days journey from their homes.

They all trooped on board, along with friends and relations. They

Icelandic cattle are the most efficient converters of grass into milk of any European breed. Photo with permission from the Icelandic Livestock Breeds. O. Dyrmundsson.

Emigrants on board S/S *Camoens*, She was known to have taken 960 to Scotland on one trip. From the newspaper HEIMKRINGLA.

had big bundles, all inside blankets, which in turn were secured firmly with rope. Apparently, they had been advised to take as much rope as possible, because it was invaluable in the New World, for tying up hay and dragging wood...

There was one family, who seemed to be much better off and it turned out that the father was a ministers son who had been to Copenhagen to study as a teacher. Karl was one of the few who spoke English and kindly offered to act as translator. He had obviously assumed the role of leader, which was good for them and us to have somebody to shoulder the responsibility. He had returned to marry his childhood sweetheart and had two young boys, one just a toddler. Karl said that it had been a heart wrenching decision. They were doing it for the sake of their children. They could not see any great future in this part of Iceland. But the farewell from their family and neighbours, who were in reality one big happy family was very distressing, especially for his wife, Anthea.

They had two big trunks. One contained tools and was obviously very heavy. They were wearing sheepskin shoes. Karl said they had been told that in America shoes and clothes were made of buffalo skin, but when wet the skin went hard, so sheep skin shoes were better. Anthea carried a spinning wheel, wrapped in a blanket . She told us that there were wool-carding combs in the tool box.

Captain Robertson had told me that he wanted to use the tide as much as possible and did not want to tarry too long. I explained the situation to Karl, who then went and told his fellow travellers.

"It is worse for the women, or do we men try not to show our emotions?" said Karl. "Some of my neighbours are coming too, so that is good for the children. They don't really understand and will soon make friends in their new home. That was one of the reasons we decided to go now, as the later we left it, the harder it would be for them."

"John Coghill, who I believe you know, tells me that two of the women are pregnant, is that right?" I asked.

"Yes, in fact, one is my wife, Anthea. But she is very hardy and as she says, she will be forced to rest as there is not much to do on board and she is a good sailor, so I have no fears. But Bergthora, I am worried about. It looks as if she could give birth on the voyage, in about a month, I think. That will be about when we land in Canada. She is not the strongest, and I believe she had a difficult birth with her first."

"By good chance we have a young doctor, on board." I said, "Although Vaughan has only the basic first aid equipment with him, it will give her assurance for this part of the journey at least. He is on holiday, but if there is an emergency he has the knowledge."

Karl went over to one family, who were very reluctant to make their final farewells. Putting his arms round them for a few moments, he then persuaded the two women who were staying to leave the boat. One of the women handed over a large package of tobacco. The American chewing tobacco was very sweet and those that had gone before resorted to smoking. The other woman handed over some money.

"They have been advised to take English money " said Karl but seeing my questioning look "Or Scottish, madam. Anyway better than Danish as the exchange rate was so much better."

We were no more than quarter of an hour tied up, when we cast off again. It was perhaps a blessing, in that the farewells were necessarily short. The emigrants were all lined around the stern waving to the few friends on the quay-side. Some of the women were obviously upset but trying not to show it for the sake of the children, who were now exploring the ship and quite oblivious to this momentous occasion in their young lives. I have to admit to a lump in my throat myself. It was after we had negotiated the sand-banks and on course down the centre of the fjord that Captain Robertson appeared on deck.

"I seenk I'll have that dram now, Mr Sleemon." said the good Captain obviously relieved that Husavik was disappearing from sight.

Robert went below and returned with a bottle of whisky and a glass. He proceeded to offer everyone on deck a dram including, all our new passengers. The Icelanders were hesitant at first, but when Karl assured them what it was, a few of the men knocked back the glass, with a cry of "Skol." The screwed up expression on their faces was followed by a surprised smile of satisfaction, and rubbing their stomachs as they felt the amber nectar having its effect.

I noticed that the women must still be below deck, presumably arranging their bedding. I went down to see how they were getting on. When after the outward journey, all the freight had been discharged, bunks were installed along one side. As there were comparatively few on this trip it was no problem, but on other trips every square inch of floor space was taken. The downside on this trip was that they were to have horses as fellow passengers. The stench, I believe could be quite overwhelming. Blankets had already been laid, some with pillows. Anthea was taking the lead and got them to lay out their cutlery and crockery. One corner was being set aside for their ablutions, with soap basin and wash tub. Each family seemed to have a chamber-pot. I said to Anthea how impressed I was with her organisation and left them to it, feeling my presence unnecessary.

For the rest of the day I was involved in packing our own cases. We would be disembarking at Akureyri to accompany John Coghill around some of the farms buying their sheep for transportation on the return of the *Camoens*. I was looking forward to this part of the trip, meeting the country folk and seeing how my husband's business was conducted.

I was just finishing off and looking forward to a cup of tea on deck, when Robert came in.

"Ewan is not too good. He's got it into his head that I am after him and he's got himself stuck in the ventilation shaft. Perhaps if you could come and talk to him, he will stop resisting against being pulled out. I think he sees you as his mother."

"Oh, poor Ewan," I said. "Of course I will come. I had so hoped that afternoon on the deck had cured him."

On reaching Ewan's cabin, I heard Vaughan talking to Ewan about the weather and how we would soon be in Akureyri and how it would be great seeing the horses loaded.

"And I should be there helping" said a muffled voice, "if I am not, he will put me into the fire. I know he will".

"Nonsense." replied Vaughan, "Here is Mrs Slimon, she will assure you that that is not so."

Vaughan squeezed passed me so that I could get nearer. Ewan's head and shoulders were stuck into the narrow opening and Jim was sitting on the bed looking worried.

"Good day, Ewan," I said, in what I hope was a motherly voice. "I just heard what you said and I have just been speaking to my husband. I can assure you he would love to see you up on deck doing your hornpipe for the emigrants. They need cheering up after leaving their families. I am sure they will have never seen a hornpipe before."

"Silence. " Would you do that just for me, Ewan, please? Just to see the smiles on the Icelanders faces would make me happy and I am sure you too."

"Will Mr Slimon be there?" asked Ewan, in a small voice.

"Not if you don't want him." I said.

"No, I would like him to be there," said Ewan. "So that he can see me doing some good. But you stay with him so that he does not touch me. Promise me that."

"I promise you, Ewan." I said. "I know Robert will be very pleased."

Jim helped Ewan out of the shaft. His head was covered in cobwebs and dust. But we cleaned him up and then led him onto the deck.

I was a bit wary, as he wasn't in the same happy frame of mind of the last performance. Vaughan suggested he get his fiddle. I was not sure about that. It was to be Ewan making the people happy. The children were running about the deck playing hide and seek when we came up. I stuck close to Ewan and asked Vaughan to fetch Robert as well and to tell him to stay beside me. Also to keep the Captain away as he might bring bad memories to Ewan.

When Ewan saw the children his face lit up immediately, and made to chase them. Then he seemed to remember what he was there for and started dancing round the deck. Soon he became totally engrossed, as if carried away by his own feet. Vaughan started playing, softly at first and then louder. The youngsters started to dance about trying to copy Ewan's intricate footwork. This obviously pleased Ewan, who put even more vim into his dancing. Some of the men got up and danced with the children and followed Ewan round. The women started clapping in time.

"Well done, dear." said Robert beside me. "We should get you a job in the asylum."

At last, Ewan with a leap in the air brought his performance to a finish. With a deep bow he accepted the loud applause with a grin from ear to ear. Robert was applauding as loud as he could. I went over and sat with Ewan while he got his breath back. Some of the children came over and sat at his feet, pleading for him to do more. This of course in Icelandic, but Ewan understood quite well want they wanted.

I did not know what to do next with Ewan to keep him in a good mood, when up got Karl and started singing a bright little Icelandic tune. Obviously a well known one as he soon had all the children joining in the chorus. Vaughan picked up the tune and started playing.

I noticed Ewan's foot tapping away in time to the music. Karl then got the children to sing a song which he explained 'to the foreigners' was a Christmas carol.

Somebody asked Vaughan to play the "Blue Danube". Again the Icelanders got up and waltzed around the deck.

I took Ewan up and we joined in. "See Ewan," I said, "You've made everybody happy. The Icelanders were very impressed. They had never seen a hornpipe danced before."

When the music stopped, I guided Ewan to the gangway. "I noticed Agnes going off to start the tea. She likes everybody to be sitting waiting for her. We had better not be late."

"Aye she's a braw lass Agnes. "said Ewan. "Goad, am I no famished. I dinna think I've eaten onything the day, ye ken. Ah could eat a horse" He started to laugh. "Maybe ye better no take they horses on board or I micht eat them a' masel." And he started to laugh again.

As we approached the cabin door, Jeannie was coming from the other direction with a tray covered with a cloth. "Aw, if its naw ma wee Jeannie." said Ewan, "Whit hiv ye got for us the day, hen"

"Its yer favourite. Fish pie." said Jeannie. A small dark not unattractive eighteen year old, whose parents hailed from the Mearns. "Ye can tak it in yersel. We're rin aff oor feet back there. Mind Jim's is there an a'. Whaur is he onywye?"

"Never you mind aboot Jim." said Ewan "I'll see he gets it. Ah think ye fancy Jim, Jeannie. Ah ken he fancies you. But you would be far better aff wi me, would she no, Mrs Slimon?"

A flush appeared on Jeannie's face as she turned and went back to the galley.

"You tuck into your pie and I'll go and get Jim," I said. "He was talking to some of the Icelandic children."

The next morning saw us sailing up the longest fjord in Iceland, Eyjafjordur, to Akureyri to pick up three hundred horses. From a long way up the fjord, John Coghill had his telescope fixed on the pier, and as we drew nearer he was trying to count the horses. They were all lined up with their owners, who were in a huddle watching our approach.

Others must have been observing our approach as well, because as we drew nearer two Danish flags were hoisted above a warehouse and a smaller building, the harbourmasters office.

"That'll be for our benefit," said Robert. "To show who's boss, by their way of it."

"It looks as if 'ey are all there," said John lowering his glass, relief in his voice. "Some of 'em have a forty mile journey from Myvatin and 'ey don't want to be away from home at this time of year longer than is necessary. It is good weather to secure the hay so it is not easy. But I think 'ey are well ahead with the good weather that we have had."

In no time we were tied up and virtually everybody trooped off and walked into Akureyri, including the emigrants, for many of whom this was to be their first experience of a town. Robert and John were to oversee the loading and I walked with George past the whaling station as fast as we could. The smell was far stronger today. Much more so than on our previous visit, as there was no wind to take away the stench.

I first went to the address where clothes were to be handed out to the emigrants. Most of them were already there and they were laughing at each other as they tried on jackets, trousers and even hats. I found the woman who seemed to be in charge. Her husband was the owner of the whaling station. I told her how appreciative we were and that it would make a big difference to the emigrants comfort. After a visit to the Apothecary, where I got some toiletries, I met George for coffee. Angus appeared from the opposite direction, in company with Agnes, the stewardess that he seemed to have struck up a relationship with. I think, in fact, she saw him as another passenger whom she was responsible for. I invited them to join us.

"Ah weel we're on the last lap now," said Angus, sinking down on a chair with a long sigh. "Is it no me that'll be glad to see Leith?"

"You have done very well, Angus," I said. "We are all eternally grateful to you for stepping into the breech at short notice."

"Aye, aye, you have all been very good to me. Sometimes I am seenking I'm a passenger ma'sel." replied Angus, with a wee glance at Agnes, who replied with a shy smile.

"I have to say Angus and you, Agnes, that I have sailed all over the world and I have never experienced such a homely and relaxed atmosphere," said George. "You have made us Sassenachs feel really at home, as if it was just one big happy family. But I think too that that comes from the top. In Captain Robertson, you have a man, who is not only an excellent seaman, keeping a tight ship but also a happy and caring ship. How you coped with poor Ewan is evidence of that."

"Aye, poor Ewan what will happen to him?'" asked Angus.

I waited for the waitress to place the coffee pot, cups and cakes on the table before replying. "We have managed to make contact with his family and hopefully one of them will be at Granton to take care of him. Apparently there is a history of mental illness in the family. How was he this morning, Agnes. Did you give him his breakfast?"

"Naw, Mam, it wis Jeannie,' said Agnes. "But she said he wis awfy quiet but also that he wis guy hungry and asked for more when she went back in."

"Well, I think that must be a good sign," I said, "I do hope you have no more problems with him."

"There's that poor wifie and her man that came on at Bordeyri,'" said Angus pointing. "They must have got their new clothes. She looks ten times better."

I turned to see Bergthora and her husband, take the only spare table, albeit they had to sit on a very rough looking bench which was far too low for the table. There was no ventilation and what with pipe smoke and the clothes of some of the customers, the pungent atmosphere overwhelmed the powerful aroma of the coffee.

Robert had given the emigrants a voucher for a meal so that they would enjoy Akureyri. He also wanted them out of the way when loading the horses. The proprietor was happy to oblige. Robert felt that, at least it would give them a good memory to leave their homeland with. He could do this with the small number we had on board this time but on occasion the *Camoens* had carried over seven hundred.

George Sim remarked on Robert's generosity and asked how the *Camoens* coped with seven hundred.

"It is not easy". I said. "Obviously, we would like to be able to give them some comfort but they are just grateful to get out. Their expectation is that this is a small price to pay for their long term benefit. Just remember the conditions we sent our own folk out to Australia in, a much longer journey, a few years ago. My father-in-law had a pair of trousers stolen from the washing line, not even new ones, but patched. That's how he was able to identify them. The wretched girl, only seventeen she was, was sent to Australia for her misdemeanour"

"I know", said George, "When I was in Australia, the stories I heard made be feel embarrassed to be English. Not just the boat journey but how the prisoners were treated, or those that survived, when they got there. We claim to be the greatest nation on earth, but these poor folk sitting over there have more reason for pride than I. They have survived for a thousand years in this country where all the elements on earth conspire against you. Fire, earthquakes, ice, snow, wind and water. They take it all in their stride. A different attitude to the New Zealanders. For them earthquakes are horrific tragedies that are quite new to them."

"I think our table might be needed," I said, as there appeared to be a queue forming at the door-way. "We'll brave the whaling station again."

"Ach, that smells no bad, at all, at all," said Angus, heaving himself off the chair with a helping hand from Agnes. "You should come to the islands,. Everybody is at the seals."

Be that as it may, we walked as briskly as we could back to the boat, leaving Angus and Agnes, who were obviously enjoying each others company, to find their own way back.

The loading was progressing well and we stopped to watch the proceedings. Each horse was put into a sling and hoisted high above the ship before being lowered into the hold and tethered alongside its mates. John had said they kept each farmers horses together as they knew each other and this helped reduce the stress. Usually they would be on the deck as well, but as we had passengers as well as emigrants, and just three hundred horses, there was no need for the deck to be used. Before loading commenced, barrow-loads of sand had been wheeled on board and spread to a depth of nine inches so that the horses would not slip. George timed each animal and declared it to be about a minute per beast, which he thought to be very impressive..

We discussed what the future of these beautiful beasts would be. Having seen them in their native environment, wide open spaces with often gale force wind, rain and snow to contend with. Yet they were so much a part of it. I wondered how they would adapt to the total opposite. Underground in dust and damp, pulling endless trucks of coal. Freedom to slavery.

George had sympathy with my views but he had seen them around the Yorkshire mines. As far as one could tell they were happy at their work. The men who tended them did so with great pride and devotion.

The horses lived and worked to a good age. In many cases they had taken over from children and that surely must be a good thing.

As he was finishing his explanation, Robert strolled over to join us. "Won't be long now," he said. "Here comes Angus and Agnes, don't they make a happy couple?"

We turned to see Angus obviously telling some story, to which Agnes was hardly able to walk for laughing. "What nonsense are you telling Agnes now?" said Robert.

"Not nonsense, at all, at all." laughed Angus. " I was chust telling Agnes that if she came back with me to the Islands, I could be teaching her all the ways of the croft. How to cut the peats, milk the cow, grow the tatties, spin and waulk the tweed and when that's done we would go out with the boat and catch the feesh for our tea."

"And no doubt it would be Agnes that would be doing the rowing," said Robert.

"Of course. I would have to teach her that as well." replied Angus. "But she is young, fit and strong and laying the lines is a skilled job, you see. Just knowing where the feesh are, you see"

"And can you pay Agnes to do all this work?" asked Robert.

"Ach, what would she be needing money for?" retorted Angus. "She would have all that any woman needs and myself for company. That right, Agnes?"

"Aye and the rain and gales and living in yin o' yer smoky blackhooses, is no fer me." laughed Agnes. "Whit wid I be giving up a good job and my family to live on a barren island with an auld cratur like you, ye auld daftie."

A shout from the ship, drew our attention. Normally it would have been the horn but the Captain would not want to give the horses a start. Captain Robertson indicated that the loading was complete. All the emigrants, many of them in their new finery were waiting to board the *Camoens*. They looked a much happier bunch than had trooped aboard in Bordeyri. It is wonderful what being warm and a full belly does to the spirit.

We said our farewells to the Misses Alex and Joan, Vaughan and George, promising to keep in touch. Miss Joan reminding me, with a shy smile, to arrange that trip to the Bass Rock. They had obviously enjoyed what was they said a unique experience. Captain Robertson appeared with a bottle of rum. A toast was drunk to a safe journey and we then waved farewell to our new friends who lined the railings alongside the group of emigrants, who had set foot on Iceland for the last time. By tomorrow their homeland would have disappeared for ever.

CHAPTER 9

LAKE MYVATIN HAYMAKING CHURCH AND GREBES

We, along with John Coghill, had booked into the hostelry in Akureyri for the night. John had arranged horses for us. John had his own three. One carrying his personal box plus a box to carry the money for the farmers. Robert and I had four between us. Two for riding one for our luggage and one spare. We had fairly long distances to travel and apparently the tracks were not the best.

When we arrived at the inn, several of the farmers were having a meal before they made their way home. They were all in good spirits having been paid by John for their horses and when he walked in a cheer went up. A bottle and glasses were passed round and a toast was made to John. John, in turn made a small hesitant speech in Icelandic and made a toast firstly to the hard working farmers of Iceland and then to Robert and myself.

Robert had invited Mr Stefansson and his wife to dinner. They arrived in the middle of John's toast, so Robert then took the opportunity of toasting Mr Stefansson, hailing him as the mayor of Akureyri, much to his embarrassment. But by the cheer that went up he seemed a very popular character. It was past midnight before the last of the revellers made for home. Their sturdy little horses were pointed in the right direction and given the Icelandic word , *baer* for home or farm and off they would go.

Our first destination was Lake Myvatin, some sixty miles to the south-east, a two day trip. John had farms to visit to pay for their horses and he liked to view and advise as to which horses he might wish to purchase the following year. Such were the distances he had to travel, only a yearly visit was possible. The horses he purchased were all three to five year old, so unless it was a very severe winter, when they could lose a lot of condition, he knew what would be waiting at the quayside next year. This would be the last inland horse trip of the year. The end of the summer was approaching and now he had to to concentrate on sheep for the autumn sailings.

I was content that day to bring up the rear whilst Robert and John discussed their programme for the days ahead.

Our stay that night was a small farm close to Godafoss. This waterfall, whilst not as impressive as Gulfoss, holds an important place in Icelandic history. A thousand years ago when they had to decide between Paganism and Christianity, their leader threw all the Pagan symbols into the waterfall. Hence its name.

This farm was to be the poorest that we stayed in on all of our trip, but I'm afraid not untypical of the Icelandic farm or croft. The entrance was the same one that was used by the cows. At this time of year the cattle were still grazing down by the rough ground at the river. John told me of some of his early summer trips where the cattle were still too weak to go outside and all the winters dung had accumulated. The smell of urine could be overpowering and the passageway in wet weather was a trial in itself.

After a cup of coffee with the farmers wife, who I have to say was not the cleanest we had met. Her clothes as well as her face were at best grimy and the two little toddlers were equally so, but they were obviously well fed and running about as happy as the day was long, but this was towards the end of summer when food was plentiful. Come the spring after a long cold winter when feed was running low and the cow was not giving milk, they could be reduced to surviving on tallow and cod liver oil.

Robert and I wandered down to the waterfall and sat for a while mesmerised by the sheer power and noise of the water. John meanwhile had gone to where some horses were grazing and met up with the farmer and two older children, who had come up from a field beside the river. The farmer was carrying a scythe. We could see the patch of grass that he had been cutting above the waterfall.

"That looks like a Scottish scythe, that he is carrying," said Robert. "I think we should go and meet him. How is your Icelandic, for by the gesticulations John is making, the farmer has not much English? It seems that the kids are acting as interpreters,"

"Well, it is certainly not as good as yours or Johns. I feel a bit guilty that I have not learnt more. Miss Wright was very good on our trip and we tended to rely on her when there was a misunderstanding. Of course, it was German that she spoke, but so many of the Icelanders speak German that that is no problem for them. You say Scottish scythe. I didn't know we had one different to others,"

"An Icelander had seen one being used in East Lothian somewhere and been so impressed, he had taken some back with him. It was the same man who initiated the start of their agricultural college. The scythes can cut double what they managed with their old type, which obviously makes a huge difference, particularly in a bad summer when there are few opportunities to make hay."

When we approached the horses were nuzzling up to the children, obviously expecting a little treat.

"I was just telling Eidur that he has some good horses and I would like to book four for next year." said John.

Eidur was clearly delighted with this bit of good news.

After a meal of dried cold fish, flour cakes, ryebread and butter and curds rather than skyr.-Robert and John sat outside smoking their pipes. The mother was putting the toddlers to bed, so she seemed pleased that I was entertaining her other children.

A violent thunderstorm drove the men inside. It struck me that at home we would have heard the rain, but such was the thickness of the turf walls that not a sound penetrated. Eidur appeared taking off his jacket as it was soaked and hung it on a hook at the side of the fire to dry. The children asked their father to read to them.

Eidur got them to sit down and John asked if we could listen as well as he thought Robert and I should experience this bit of Icelandic culture. He said that although he could not understand what was being said he enjoyed just being in a setting that had not changed for several hundred years. The Sagas being passed down from generation to generation. The stories of six or seven hundred years ago were told as if it were yesterday. They were hearing tales of their ancestors as if it were their grandparents.

Farmstead in winter. Sheep are generally wintered inside. Photo with permission to the author of the Reykjavik Photographic Museum.

Horses are out-wintered.' (Vikings. picture by E.Douglas.)

Eidur waited for his wife to finish putting the toddlers down and we could hear her telling a story to the wee ones. Eidur had the book in his hand and John asked if we could look at it. It was, explained John, made of calfskin and could be many hundred years old. The quills that they had used were that of ravens or swans and the ink made from the bearberry plants. Not surprisingly, the books were very expensive to make, yet every household had one.

The light over Eidur's head was no better than a candle. The children sat crossed-legged at their fathers feet, taking in every word. It reminded me of my own upbringing, the difference being that we were told fairy tales and later make believe adventure like those being written at present by H Rider Haggard. These children were hearing their own family history. The troubles and strife as well as romance, down through the ages. It made me think how ignorant I was of my own family background and I suddenly felt privileged to witness this age-old tradition in being. This was true family. .

`After perhaps three quarters of an hour, Eidur suddenly came to a close and he then said a short prayer. He got up to put the book away and hugged his little ones goodnight.

I, too, said "Godda not". The next morning the thunderstorm had cleared away and another fine day was promising with the sun already high in the sky as we said fond farewells to Eidur and his family.

In the early afternoon, John pointed out the columns of steam away in the distance as our destination. We were following the river Laxa which was one of many that flowed into Lake Myvatin. Not long after we came in sight of the Lake, stretching between us and the sulphur springs.

As we were approaching a farmstead, a rather unpleasant smell reached us and as we passed we saw the reason. At the back of the farm, three men were skinning some sheep. One was pulling the skin off a beast hanging from a frame, while another was skinning a sheep in a cradle frame, whilst a third was butchering on a table. John went over and had a quick word. This was the local autumn kill apparently.

Lake Myvatin, according to John, is one of the driest areas of Iceland, but because of the fertile warm water, also one of the worst for midges. But again because of the midges there are huge numbers of birds, particularly ducks. In fact, other than Lake Thingvellavatn it is the only place where midges are to be found in Iceland.

A bigger variety of ducks are to be found here than anywhere else in the country. As we neared the lake, this became apparent. In parts, one could hardly see the water for these busy birds, diving, standing flapping their wings, chasing after each other. I was able to identify quite a number for I used to frequent Aberlady Bay to the East of Edinburgh. One that I was thrilled to spot was the long-tailed duck. I had seen them at Aberlady on two occasions, but here they were in abundance. Then just as I realised I was holding the men back, I noticed the Icelandic speciality, the harlequin duck. This brightly coloured little duck, held me spellbound. Oh, how I wish I could paint! Magnus had told me he was sure that Jemima Blackburn had painted one and I made a mental note to find her painting on my return. Apparently the harlequin depends on midges through the nesting season as does the Barrows goldeneye. I saw goldeneye but was not expert enough to tell it from the ordinary goldeneye. If I had thought I might have borrowed Johns telescope. But then it is not the best instrument for bird watching. At last, I turned away only to find Robert and John had dismounted and John had lit his pipe to keep the midges away. Thankfully there was quite a strong breeze. John, ever the gentleman, just told me to take my time. He appreciated that this was a special place and that it meant a lot to me to experience it. Robert, who had good knowledge of farmland and woodland birds going back to his childhood on the farm of South Gyle farm west of Corstorphine and before that in the Lanarkshire village of Carnwath, came wandering over to share in my pleasure. I was able to identify at least half a dozen different ducks from where we stood.

Eventually with the horses finding the flies too much for them, we proceeded on our way. We were going to stay three nights at the next farm, as John was going about twenty miles east to another farm to view sheep and ponies. So he suggested I could spend the day going to the other side of the lake which was even more densely populated with birds. This seemed like a good plan to me.

After a breakfast of porridge, black pudding, ryebread and lashings of coffee, Margret indicated that she would be happy to have me help her turn the hay. She gave Robert and John a parcel of black pudding and ryebread for their journey.

Margret, seemed so pleased that I was able to spend the day there and had very good English, that she assumed she was going to entertain me by demonstrating her skills at making Skyr knitting and turning their hay. They had no family and I perceived Margret was lonely. So I ended up helping her with her washing at a nearby spring. By the time that was finished, the hay was dry enough to turn after the morning dew. So we helped her husband, Bjorn, turn hay in one field and then make little coles in another. Margret had taken cheese, bread and milk for our midday meal and I have to say I was ready for it not being used to such physical work. Margret had asked me to carry her knitting, so that after eating our 'piece' she started knitting, at the same time relating about her own background. I was struggling to keep awake in the warmth of the sun. We turned the hay again and then made for home whilst Bjorn went to cut more hay.

It was trout for supper and `Robert and John arrived in high good spirits at the same time as Bjorn arrived back from his days labour. John produced a bottle of corn brandy and it seemed to have a powerful effect for in no time Bjorn was chattering away, obviously relating what a successful day it had been and what a difference I had made.

Apparently the farmer in the interior was so pleased with the prices John had offered him that after pouring them all a few drinks, he had presented John and Robert with a bottle each.

Robert was fascinated to meet another man, a shepherd, who had come from deep in the interior with some of the farmer's sheep. Apparently he lived about forty miles from the nearest habitation and spent his time going into the remotest places where sheep might wander and then returning them to the farmers for a small payment per head. Because of the extreme difficulty of the country he spent the summer months climbing over ranges of mountains and herding the sheep back to the valleys, where the shepherds could gather them in the autumn sheep drives.

The next morning was the Sabbath and the whole family were going to church and Margret made it plain that she would be delighted if we joined the family at worship. I was a bit hesitant in going to a Lutheran church but from what I had gathered they were not unlike our own and it was as much a social occasion as strictly religious. Robert said he would like to join us and assured me that I would appreciate the service even although in a foreign tongue. He had been on a previous trip and the singing was worth it on its own.

Margret wore the traditional Icelandic dress, whilst Bjorn appeared in a smart suit. Robert assured me that a smart skirt and blouse would be most appropriate. It was one that I wore on board ship.

We rode the two miles and I was feeling very stiff with the exertions of the previous day but pleasantly so in that I felt I had been of real use for the first time on this trip. We were joined on the way by another family from further up the valley, whose teenage sons came galloping up to catch us and then after being introduced queried Bjorn on the progress of the hay season. In the meanwhile Margret told me the extraordinary story of the church in which we were going to worship.

The church was in the little village of Reykjahlid. In 1727 there was huge volcanic activity at Krafla and the Leirhnjukur crater sent streams of lava the eight miles towards Lake Myvatin. In 1729 the lava reached the village, ploughing through it and surrounding farms but the wooden church which sat on a small rise was amazingly saved. Some said it was a miracle, the lava flow parting and missing it by a few yards. It was rebuilt on its original foundation in1876. Margret said she would show me the wooden carving of the original church on the pulpit after the service.

People were mingling in front of the church, the minister amongst them. Most were in their 'Sunday Best' . It is the womenfolk and in particular two with blond hair, blue eyes and clear pale skins that are worthy of description. Their fair hair was braided into long plaits, turned up to form two loops crossed on the crown of the head. On top of the braids was a little black silk knitted cap. It fitted close to the head like an inverted saucer. It was secured to the head by silver pins. Hanging from this cap was a thick black tassel, about eight inches long. At the top, the tassel passed through a silver tube of very fine workmanship. The bodices were pretty, bound two inches wide with black velvet. It was joined at the waist and neck with silver buckles. The bust was left open, showing a white shirt embroidered with the finest stitch. The skirt was short and full and made of black cloth. Margret, who was dressed a bit more simply, noticed my admiring looks and asked if I might like an introduction. The girls spoke good English and they allowed me to inspect the embroidery , which was really exquisite and they explained had been made by their granny. I had seen them in a shop in Reykjavik, but it was only when seen on the heads of these 'models' that their beauty struck home...

Margret introduced me to the minister. Sven was a serious looking man of middle years and a warm handshake. His English was excellent as he asked me if Robert was my husband and he would very much like to meet him, as he had heard and read so much about him. I disentangled Robert from a group of Bjorn's farming friends and brought him over to Sven.

"I am very honoured to meet you, Mr Slimon." said Sven. "Your business has done so much for our people. When they see adequate reward for their labours it does so much for their spirit as well as their material comforts. The one feeds off the other."

Robert was flattered and said so...

He was interrupted by one of the senior residents, who was pointing to his watch indicating that the Service should be started.

We filed into the simple building and sat next to Bjorn and Margret. Perhaps there were another twenty five people, mostly elderly. There was a picture of a boat behind the pulpit. In the boat was, presumably, Christ and his disciples in a stormy sea.

The minister very kindly welcomed us in English before announcing the first hymn. Robert was right. The singing was beautiful. Margret, standing beside me, had a very strong voice. I was perhaps pleased that I could not read Icelandic as it gave me adequate excuse not to sing. The sermon was not very long by Scottish standards and soon the minister was saying a benediction. Margret showed Robert and I the fine carving on the pulpit, before going out into the bright midday sun. After more exchanges of news Bjorn suggested we ride along the other side of the lake to a neighbouring farmer for coffee. The farmer seemed genuinely pleased when Bjorn suggested this. I had been given the impression that the Icelanders were not the most religious of people and that the Sunday service was as much a social occasion. This experience served only to strengthen that feeling. Many of these people lived very lonely lives and would look forward to Sundays to catch up with all the local news. It seemed that there were quite a few of the further travelled going to visit their friends who lived nearer to the church.

We all mounted and trotted along getting into the ,tolt' or the fifth gait as it sometimes called. Apparently it is a characteristic also common

Securing hay for transportation. Photo with permission to the author of the Reykjavik Photographic Museum.

Hay transport. In hard times hay is everything. Photo with permission to the author of the Reykjavik Photographic Museum.

to Mongolian breeds. I found it difficult back at Geyser, but today on a better road and a level surface I found it quite exhilarating.

"You will be able to see more of the ducks from here". said Margret, as we came to a little rise. And so we did. It was simply amazing. The sheer mass of numbers. Of course, this was when they were at their maximum numbers with all the young hatched and almost ready for the long flight South.

"Look up there." said Robert pointing. "A gyr falcon. I have only seen one before and it cannot be anything else as it is the only falcon they have."

"Oh, magnificent. That has really made my day." I said as we watched this beautiful bird soar over the lake and then fly off in the direction from which we had come.

Soon we arrived at the farm. They had a little verandah overlooking the lake where we sat with our coffee. The farmer wanted to show Robert his stock. He seemed particularly proud of his cows. I said I would be more than happy to just sit and watch the birds whilst Margret and the farmers wife,whose name sounded like Helen, caught up with each others news. The farmer lent me a pair of very good binoculars and I spent the next half hour totally enthralled. My chair faced out over the lake, but to the left was a little bay with an island, perhaps thirty yards diameter. I was just putting the binoculars on the table to my left, when something caught my eye. I looked up and sailing out from behind the island was a Great Northern Diver with two little ones in tow. I could not believe it. I grabbed the binoculars and focussed excitedly on the three majestic birds. They were, perhaps, just a hundred yards away and I wanted to shout to Margret but was frightened to do so or move, otherwise the 'Loons', as they are called in America might take off. I was certain they were 'Loons' as our host had pictures of all the various species that might be seen from the verandah along one wall and pride of place was given to the Great Northern Diver.

I sat watching these beautiful birds, with their long pretty coloured black and white necks, wishing again that I had the ability to paint. The whole scene was just perfect. They had just turned and disappeared behind their island when Margret came through with our hostess. I started babbling out what I had just seen and in my excitement forgot that I was speaking to two people whose English was good but not good enough to understand what must have seemed like a lunatic. I went over to the picture on the wall and then pointed at the island.

"Mother and two chicks, ducklings or whatever." I said excitedly.

"Ah, the Loons! The Loons." exclaimed Helen, " They still here? We thought they must have gone South. We have not seen them for a few days. Oh, I am so glad you see them . They are beautiful, yes?"

"Yes, indeed." I agreed.

"Look, here come the men." said Margret.

"Ah, yes. We must have a toast to the loons." laughed Helen and off she scurried and came back with a bottle of schnapps and glasses.

While she filled the glasses I repeated my tale to Robert.

So we raised our glasses "Skal! To the Loons!"

"Do you know," said Robert, "Although the divers winter with us and other parts of Europe, Iceland is the only place where they nest. Wise birds."

At this time of year the Icelanders had another harvest to gather, the berries. On our journey we had noticed families at the side of the tracks bent over busily filling their cans and bags. Today it was our turn. John had suggested he would meet us at a burn where he would have a brew up waiting. True to his word we could see the smoke from his fire curling up into overcast sky and as we neared the little bridge we smelt the mutton chops.

John was showing another side to his character. An expert chef. He had a creamy wildberry sauce and red cabbage cooking gently in a pan.

"I thought I would have to eat it all myself if you weren't coming. What kept you, was the sermon too long?" asked John, as he took the top off a bottle of schnapps and started pouring it into teacups and passing them round.

"Skal" said John before downing his cupful.

Bjorn apologised saying it was his idea to go and have coffee. I interjected saying that it had been well worth it seeing both gyr falcon and the divers.

"Ah well you had better tuck in before it gets burnt." said John adding more dwarf birch to the fire. "I made the sauce with some of the berries that I picked. I'll go and put on the billy can for coffee" Off he went to the burn to get water.

Icelandic traditional dress. Photo by the author.

Nearly all Icelanders are Lutheran. Photo by the author.

"This is first class, John" shouted Robert after him as he tucked into a succulent chop. "We'll not be able to bend to pick berries after this lot."

However, bend we did and filled all the boxes and bags that John had brought the food in. The wild berries were big and juicy and easy to pick. John made another brew, before we made our way home after a most satisfying day.

CHAPTER 10

HUSAVIK AND THE LOST SILVER

It was thirty six miles to Husavik, our next farm-stay and what a disappointing trail it was. We climbed up to the North for two or three miles and looking back at a short stop, I again wished I had the ability to draw. The scene looking over Lake Myvatin was exquisite in the morning sun with the glacial mountains away in the distance. Looking over to the east, I could just make out Bjorn and his wife turning the hay, It would be a great day for it, because as John remarked there was a good drying breeze.

The next ten or so miles was as barren a stretch of land as I had experienced but John assured me it was nothing to some of the interior with its lava beds, which in places were all but impassable. Gradually the land became greener and the occasional farm was passed.

A big bay called Skjalfandi appeared in the distance and the sight of it was signal for our midday stop. We sheltered behind a big rock while the horses enjoyed a bite of grass beside a burn. John passed around his bottle of corn brandy persuading me to take a draught for my still aching bones. Two delicious sandwiches of smoked mutton followed by some chocolate that Vaughan had given us completed the meal. Food always tastes better out in the fresh air and I confess I snoozed off for five minutes. The last two nights had not been the most comfortable, as the room was particularly airless, so I had not had the best of sleeps.

As we rode alongside increasingly fertile land and bigger farms, Robert and John recalled how they came to bring the farmers together to encourage them to build a pier to enable the *Camoens* and other boats to Husavik. There was a big number of prime stock in the area and it was of advantage to all if a pier could be built. The Icelanders had been so unused to developing anything of this nature on their own that when it was first suggested their reaction was that 'if you wanted it, you should build it.' Robert and John had always been impressed by the sense of community and felt they needed encouraged rather than discouraged as the Danes were wont to do. When John told them how much more he would be prepared to pay for their horses and more-so for their sheep because of the stress of the sixty mile journey, then their attitude changed remarkably. To have their goods delivered right to the quayside, particularly in rough weather could only be of advantage. Once their minds were made up, they moved with great enthusiasm and efficiency first to form a cooperative and then to organise the building of the pier. Apparently, such had been the success of this venture that soon cooperatives were springing up all over Iceland.

They realised that together they had stronger bargaining power. John encouraged them, as the bigger the numbers he could get together, the better the over all price he could offer. The farmers could also order large quantities of foods, tools or building materials.

About a mile before Husavik, John turned off the track and followed a path alongside a stream, which led to the farm of Geitar Stadir, or goats farm. Three little children came running down to meet us and John threw out his arms in welcome. They all danced round John as if he were a long lost uncle. This was the farm of their parents, Gardar and his wife Gretel, who were great friends of John.

Gardar was not at home, but was expected back from helping his neighbour make hay . Meanwhile, Gretel showed us our rooms. I think her name was Gretel, as that was what it sounded like. If she spelt it the same as in the fairy tale I cannot be sure and John did not know either. Normally John would have slept in the best room but now we had that honour. The two beds were placed end to end along one wall. there was a small window which did not open with the result that the ventilation was non existent. There was a portrait of Sira Haigrimur Petursson, the esteemed poet. He was wearing a particularly severe stare which I will have to face when lying down. The bed had no blankets. Rather they had quilts filled with the down of the eider. Very warm, light and comfortable they are. Robert found them too warm particularly in this room which was airless. There was a mirror, which I was thankful for. It was surprising how one takes little things for granted and to get up in the morning and comb ones hair without looking at oneself was very frustrating. There was also a table and chair and an American clock. The room was brightly painted blue which contrasted with John's room where the bed was no more than a bench in a room that would appear to have been used as a store rather than a bedroom.

"I think I can smell coffee" said Robert, "I could do with a bite. That was a long ride today although very enjoyable. The contrast in scenery from the bleak to fertile fields and the great views of the fiord and with John's knowledge and stories of the farms and folk that we passed, helped to make the time pass quickly "

" He really loves this country and its people, doesn't he?" I said. "You are very lucky to have him. But I suppose he is equally lucky to have you."

"Aye, it was very fortunate that he had both the experience of the sea and a great knowledge of stock." said Robert. "It was just the right challenge for him at the right time in his life. When I think of the struggle I had when importing ponies from Germany. In spite of the primitive conditions here as compared with Germany, but the big bonus too has been for the Icelanders. What a great people they are. You just want to do well for them. They have such a great attitude to life."

We went through to find Gardar had yet to return but Gretel was feeding her three children and three mugs of steaming coffee were sitting on the table. John suggested he could show us the eider ducks nesting site down by the shore. Immediately, the oldest boy said "Can we show them, Mum? We know where all the nests are." Mum spoke back in their native tongue, but with some finger wagging. She had obviously complied but pointing at the clock the children had a time limit.

This was not just a Nature Walk but a look at a commercial enterprise. It was long past the nesting season but as we approached the beach over a grassy foreshore the children were running to find the various nests first. They were all marked with two foot posts, painted green at the top. There must have been at least fifty in the hundred or so yards that we crossed and the grass stretched for a good quarter mile along the beach. John warned us to watch out for puffin nests as well. They were little burrows into which one could step and twist an ankle. The eider nests had the remnants of down in amongst the twigs and grasses. We then came to a three foot high dyke running parallel to the shore for about fifty yards and along the bottom were recesses at three foot intervals, each one had a nest. John explained that the same ducks returned year after year to the same nest.

When the ducks first make their nests by pulling the down out of their breasts, the farmer goes round and collects it in a bag. The duck repeats the process and again the farmer collects. The poor duck again replenishes the nest but this time the farmer lets it be to bring up its young as it would be detrimental to the ducks' well-being to take a further crop.

"I suppose it is not dissimilar to a wool crop to the farmer." said Robert. "He has to protect and nurture the birds, so that they breed successfully for next years crop."

"Yes, in days gone by, apparently, there was a lot of poaching and taking as much down as possible, but now it is the landowners right and it has been shown with proper protection they can flourish. On Vigur Island in the North West there are several thousand and it is the farmers main income.

"So what is it worth?" I asked.

"The last figure I heard was about 70d per lb." Robert replied. "But, of course, it takes a big volume of down to weigh a pound."

"Ah, here comes Gardar," said John, pointing to a figure striding towards us. "He will give you all the facts and figures. He's very fond of his ducks"

John introduced us to this small well built man. Unfortunately, Gardar's English was about the same standard as John's Icelandic. Gardar led us to a little inlet a short distance away where there were literally thousands of ducks and ducklings swimming around. He then produced a loaf of bread which he proceeded to feed the ducks with.

From `Johns translation we understood that he did this every night and morning. He did not want the ducks going to any of his neighbours land to nest. All this was said with a big grin, so how serious he was we were not sure, but he was obviously very passionate about his eiders. Suddenly he pointed to his farm and held up the last bit of bread indicating that it was time for us to eat. I realised that I was very hungary as we trekked back up the shore, trying to keep up with Gardars rapid pace.

Gardar led us through one of the side doors of the five that were facing us. This was the 'down room'. At the far end was a low wooden partition behind which was this years harvest.

In the middle of the floor was a wooden contraption that they used to separate out the twigs, moss and other detritus. This was a winter job, in the meantime the air was encouraged to circulate through the room to dry it.

The almost inevitable mutton stew followed by rhubarb and skyr soon satisfied my appetite. Prior to the meal John had produced a bottle of whisky. He knew how to pour a dram and insisted that I partake as well. John declaring that there was nothing better to relax the body after a hard day in the saddle or in Gardars case, the harvest field. Indeed after ten minutes or so it was hard to disagree. Whilst the lady of the house made coffee, John poured another stiff dram into the three men's glasses.

John told us that Gardar was named after the first man to settle in Iceland. Gardar Svavarsson came from Sweden around 850, a hundred years before Ingolfur Arnarson landed in Reykjavik. He built a settlement called Husavik and although he left the following spring some of his slaves remained and became the original settlers. Gardar was emphatic that this was fact and who were we to disagree?

The talk turned to the organisation of the gathering of the sheep, the reiter, and which days John would value them and where.

I turned to Gretel, "Takk fyrir mig", I said, showing that I had appreciated her meal. She smiled in return but when I offered to help with the clearing up, she was quite insistent that she would do it herself. In fact, I wondered if I were insulting her. John had said that if I had not been there she would not have dined with us, but would eat in the kitchen watching when to clear for the next course. Women seem still to be subservient although John said that in the time that he has been coming, over twenty years now, he has noticed a movement to more equality. When he first came to Iceland, it was the custom for the lady of the house not to sit at the table but at the kitchen door to make sure the next course was being prepared the way she wanted and be ready to serve it when the previous course was finished. When it came to retiring to bed she would make sure her guests were tucked up safely. A custom that John readily admitted to taking advantage of.

I had taken a little walk up the hill behind the house as I found the atmosphere somewhat claustrophobic. There was a pretty little burn with the summer flowers just beginning to fade. I sat down and enjoyed the sound of the burn and tried to identify the songs of the various birds. When I returned, there were three horses tethered in the yard. Gretel met me at the door with big grin. Their neighbours, on hearing that John was here, had come over to find out what his plans were for the sale of their sheep.

We were about to enter the house when all the men came out and went into the 'down room' which also served as a kind of local bar. Gardar was a very popular character and as his farm was central to the district, it was a natural meeting place. When Gardar had shown us the room before, I had wondered why there were benches placed round the walls. This arrangement allowed the children to get to sleep and the men to ceilidh. Gardar had a very good voice and these men were part of his 'choir' also. I went in and sat with some socks that needed darned although it was not easy in the poor light. After completing four or five, I felt my eyes getting heavy, whether through concentration or just tiredness, I excused myself to Gretel and retired to our room from where I could hear the men singing in the 'down room'. Beautiful singing it was.

I was awoken the next morning by Robert sitting on my bed. He informed me that my day had been arranged, in fact my next two days. That I was to go a two day hike with a William Lord Watts and his sister to look at the cliffs of Asberg. They were staying in near-by Husavik and had heard that we were here and invited us to come with him and his sister. Robert was going across the fjord with John to meet with the farmers who were gathering their sheep off the peninsula to Eyjafjord. They were going in the *Miaca*, a small Newcastle steamer that Robert had bought recently as a feeder vessel. The idea was that it could take small packages of sheep and act as a feeder for the *Camoens* and other boats that were chartered for the busy spell. This would allow for a quicker turnaround. In the winter it was to act as a ferry service to Norway. This gathering would take four days and we would sail round to meet them in the next fjord and load the sheep and then set off for Scotland. After meeting the farmers they were going to Bordeyri, where hopefully there would be a 'parcel' of sheep awaiting them.

"I think I will be quite ready for the *Camoens* after all this exertion." I muttered as I got out of bed. "Tell me about this Mr Watts."

"I met him last year when we gave him a lift on the Buda from Husavik to Bordeyri. That was when the *Fifeshire* had broken her propellor shaft and had to be towed into the Faroes. We chartered the *Buda* and she came out from Leith, picked up the *Fifeshire* cargo and deposited it in Akureyri We then loaded some three hundred ponies in Bordeyri and went into the Faroes and towed the *Fifeshire* home. Luckily there was a following wind otherwise we could have been struggling. " said Robert. "But back to William Watts. He is trying to develop Sulphur mining at Myvatin and other places. He is good company. An interesting man and very knowledgeable on geology. I think he may have Mr Locke of the Iceland guide book with him as well. I have to go now as there is quite a wind blowing and Gardar thinks it will get worse so we want to get across the fjord as quickly as possible. Mr Watts should be here about ten o' clock as this is on his route. Good bye for now and enjoy yourself." And with that he was gone.

Gretel was in the kitchen. "Ah, eat?" pointing to a plate of bread, cheese and meat, a bowl of skyr and a big cup of strong coffee. I sat down on a box beside the fire and tucked into my breakfast. At first I thought that Gretel was making someone else's breakfast till she started putting it in a box and placed it front of me with a big grin. I realised this was my picnic lunch for today.

"Takk, takk" I said. I was embarrassed that she was going to all this trouble. She had no doubt made boxes for Robert, John and Gardar as well, not to mention having to feed her own children.

As I was going back to my room, one of the boys came in through the door rubbing rain from his hair and face. "Rain, wind, snow." said he, disappearing down the passageway. I went to have a look myself. Robert had said that there was a wind blowing but this was a gale and horizontal rain with it. Beyond where the eider ducks nest, the fjord had white horses and the hills beyond had snow almost to the shore. My immediate thought was of the three men going across Skalfandi, but John was not called Captain for nothing. His navigation skills were as respected as his stockman expertise. Gardar had sailed these waters all his days. It was a good two hours since they left so they were probably across by now.

But this was no day to gather sheep let alone go for a horse ride. I just hoped William Lord Watts was of a like mind. I went into the 'down room' from where I could view the storm through the window. I had barely closed the door, when I saw a figure bent against the gale come round the corner of the house and through the main door. This , I presumed was Mr Watts. He was still in the passageway shaking down his cloak when I entered.

"Lord Watts?" I asked.

"Ah! You must be Mrs Slimon. Yes, I am William Watts. How do you do?." said the arrival holding out his hand. He was a big man with a black bushy beard and deep blue eyes. He had a strong Yorkshire accent, which I was to find a little difficult to follow. He hung his cloak on a nail behind the door. "What a day. It just suddenly blew up an hour ago. I know how hardy you Scots are, but I hope you don't mind if we call it off today. It would be no pleasure and although the guides are willing to go, they are not very keen."

"Not at all! Not at all!" I replied, "I must say I was hoping you would say that. We have been very lucky with the weather so far, so I can't complain about one lost day."

"Gretel had appeared. "Coffee?" she asked.

Lord Watts replied in Icelandic to the obvious delight of Gretel, who led us through to the kitchen. We perched ourselves on a bench and took the two mugs of steaming coffee proffered by our hostess.

"Ah, I was needing that." exclaimed Lord Watts.

"At least we can postpone our little adventure." I said. "It is not so easy for the shepherds, all the days are full so that John can travel from one place to another to value the sheep and if the sheep are not there to be loaded then the boat will sail on to Bordeyri and they will have to await the next sailing in ten days or a fortnight. In the meantime the sheep will have lost condition as there is limited grazing near the loading place."

"It must be quite a challenge to get the sheep all gathered at the right time and place." said Lord Watts. "I hear that Robert pays very well and that must be an incentive for the Icelanders to get their sheep ready."

"Yes, the King of the reiter, as they call him, has it very well organised.

When we were at church up at Myvatin the minister announced the times and place to meet from the pulpit. Each farmer has to send a number of men in proportion to the number of sheep that he possesses. But that is not a problem. The Icelanders so enjoy a reason to take their horses and show off their skills to their neighbours."

"Oh, they do don't they?" replied Lord Watts,taking a biscuit offered by Gretel. "Tell me. I know that these ponies go to the coal-mines, but do you get any demand for them in your Highlands for instance, or are your Scottish breeds better?"

"Well." I replied, "Some people have tried them and they are no doubt as hardy as our Highland breeds. The Highland garrons are used for carrying stags off the hills on these new Highland Estates and every thing must be Highland, the tartan, heather, whisky and,yes, the horses."

"Do I detect hint of envy?" teased William. "The Highlands are the place now to be seen and explore."

"Yes., but it is you, sir, who should be envious. There is nowhere in the rest of Britain that has such scenic grandeur." I said. "They have seen big changes this century from the seventeen hundreds, when the common conception was that it was a place for savages who ate their own children. But ,of course, that was very far from the truth. Some of the Highland chiefs and their clans had a very sophisticated way of life. This is now being recognised and idolised by the English aristocracy with her Majesty to the fore. The fact that the scenery is majestic and there happens to be a surfeit of all types of sport for the hunting, shooting fraternity, is a huge bonus."

We could hear a commotion in the passage-way, then through the door burst a figure in a state of some distress. He removed his dripping hat and cloak, all the while muttering and pointing to the door. Gretel appeared and, obviously, recognising the newcomer, started to assist him. Soon there was a pool of water on the floor. He was absolutely drenched and William rose and put his now dry coat around the poor man and almost pushed him onto a chair by the fire, where he started to remove his trousers, cow-skin boots and stockings all of which appeared to be utterly soaked. William took a towel and rubbed his legs vigorously. Gretel had put the kettle on to the heat along with a pan of stew. Then she produced a bottle of whisky, from which she poured a generous dram. What a wonderful medicine it is. Stefan, for that was what Gretel called him, drained the glass in one and immediately the colour returned to his cheeks and a big smile spread over his face. Looking round he saw me for the first time and the smile left his face. Gretel said my name and immediately, he seemed to shrink. He turned away and started talking and gesticulating to Gretel. She was having difficulty in understanding him but eventually she turned to William and spoke to him who in turn translated for me.. I was aware that Stefan was watching me with something akin to fear in his eyes. What could all this mean? Had some tragedy befallen the men crossing the Fjord?

William started to explain through a cloud of steam from Stefan's clothes, that our visitor had been coming from Reykjavik on the over-land route with a vast quantity of silver on two horses when one of the horses stumbled and injured itself. He had to leave half the silver beside the track and continue on. He was now frightened that either the money would be stolen or it would be covered in snow and he would be unable to find it. Naturally, he thought that I would be cross and feared what I might do, poor man. I got up and went over and put my arm round him and asked William to reassure him that I was pleased that he had come through the storm and that he was in no way to blame for an accident. The relief on Stefans face was almost comical and William persuaded him to eat the stew, which he did with obvious relish.

Whilst Gretel poured another steaming mug of coffee, William and I discussed what we should do. With the storm raging it was thought that Robert and John would not be back till late on the morrow at the earliest.

"Perhaps it is fortuitous that I came today, for instead of going to see the Asberg cliffs, I can be of much more use going for the silver." said William.

" But how far away is it?" I asked. "And how much money did he leave?"

William turned to Gretel and Stephan and after some gesticulation and holding up of fingers, William concluded that it was a day and a half ride away and, William calculated the silver was worth about one thousand pounds sterling. It had been packed in boxes.. The noise we had initially heard was Stephan lifting the boxes into the house.

"This is what we shall do." he said. He was obviously a man who was used to taking control of situations and enjoying it. "I shall go back to Husavik and let my sister know what is happening and shall return first thing tomorrow morning with our other two horses. They are all very sturdy . I will pick up Stephan here and he will show me where he left the money and hope to goodness that it will still be there. I know if it was in Yorkshire, it would be long gone by now,. But this is Iceland and I would place a fair bet that it will still be where it was left, even if the half of Reykjavik were to ride by. In all my dealings with Icelanders I have found them scrupulously fair and honest. Do you know a couple of years ago I left Akureyri for a weeks travel without my watch? I met a farmer and on asking him the time and explaining my stupidity, he immediately offered me his one and I arranged to leave it in the Apothecary on my return. I don't know that I would lend mine to a complete stranger ."

"It does not surprise me,. Both Robert and John have similar tales. But this seems hardly fair on you," I said. "You were going on a pleasant trip to the Asberg cliffs that you were anxious to see and now you end up going on this long trek along a road that you will have travelled many times. I am sure there must be someone that Gretel!"

"Nonsense!" interrupted William. "It will be something useful to do and I suggest you might like to have a look at Husavik with my sister. It is a pretty little place, with an interesting church. I am sure she would enjoy your company. She misses a good gossip with other women and she was so looking forward to this trip today."

"Well, yes, I would love to do that." I said. "I find it difficult at times myself, I must admit. Wonderful people that they are, we are just not the same."

"That's great," said William, getting up "I shall go now and hope this storm blows itself out . I had better make sure Stephan understands the plan." But when he looked round Stephan was fast asleep on the bench. "Poor guy he is done in. Gretel" he said raising his voice and she came scurrying in, William explained the plan to her and then with a "Bless, Bless." he was gone.

I had noticed some books in our room and for the rest of the day I got acquainted with Walter Scotts "Redgauntlet." When the light began to fade, I ventured out and although the rain had practically stopped, the wind appeared just as strong and I took a ten minute stroll as far as the bottom of the hill alongside the burn, which gave a little shelter from the gale.

Once Gretel had put the three children to bed, I persuaded her to allow me to help with darning a basket of socks. Stephan, who had slept for most of the day but had been out to bed his horses, joined us and he and Gretel talked away. They each took a dram from the whisky bottle after which they had a little ceilidh, Stephan reciting poetry, which I gathered was his own and Gretel, who had a beautiful voice, sang what sounded like lullabies.

Next morning, the storm had passed and the sun was struggling to break through a watery sky, but the snow was still lying low down the hills. True to his word, Lord Watts appeared shortly after daybreak. Stephan had been out to his ponies and decided to leave the lame one behind. I was to meet William's sister, Jane, in the church in Husavik at eleven o'clock and take a picnic. With out more ado they departed and I went to assist Gretel make up some bread and cheese. She also put in two legs of duck. I gave the children half a bar of chocolate and put the remainder in the haversack.

It was about a mile to Husavik and the church sat across the road from the pier. Typical of the churches I had seen throughout Iceland from the outside, it was a simple building. There was no one inside when I pushed open the heavy door, but I was early, as William had said there were some interesting features. There was a beautifully carved font and on either wall there were very pretty murals. I was studying the second of these when a dainty figure appeared in the doorway.

"Mrs Slimon?" said the lady. "Aren't these murals wonderful"?

"Yes, but please call me Robina." I replied. I had expected a bigger figure in line with her brothers imposing stature. But I was to learn later that she was a twin in difficult birth in which her twin had died and her mother had been ill for much of her childhood.

"And I am Jane" she replied ,holding out her white gloved hand for me to shake. "I am looking forward to our walk after being cooped up yesterday. What a day that was."

" I have to say we are very appreciative of William's very noble offer of going to collect the silver." I said.

"Oh. He just loves a challenge and being able to push himself. Have you seen these candlesticks?" she said walking across to the pulpit. " They, like the murals are thought to be sixteenth century. We are staying with the minister and he keeps us entertained with all the local history and sagas."

I agreed with her, adding that one did not expect to find such items in so remote a place.

Jane explained that there were two good walks, one of which was a three mile trek to the South up a fairly steep track to the top of the cliffs that were over twelve hundred feet high. There were two islands offshore one of which, she explained had a population of a hundred or so and tens of thousands of seabirds, puffins and fulmars mainly. It was called Lundey, the other being Flatey and not inappropriately named as it barely rose above sea level. By this time we were outside the church and Jane was pointing out the islands away to the South.

"But as you can see,"said Jane. "The snow will be deep at the top of the cliffs, so I suggest we walk around a lake, called Botnsvatn, at the back of the village. Its about three and a half miles distant. There is a pretty stream at the far end where we can have our picnic."

The rest of the day past very pleasantly, Jane being very knowledgeable about all the plants and flowers, which with yesterdays storm had a rather bedraggled look. She also had a great interest in and enthusiasm for her brothers work as a geologist. So just listening to her describe the various features of the dramatic landscape gave it a whole new meaning.

We found a little hollow covered in berries and after consuming our lunch we filled our sandwich boxes with berries without hardly moving ourselves. "Always make the day pay, is one of my by brothers favourite sayings." said Jane. "I am sure our hosts will appreciate this."

"Yes." I agreed, "They do not have much fruit or vegetables in their diet, so they really value the berries."

We continued round the lake and with the sun in our eyes we completed a very pleasant afternoon. Jane invited me in to the parsonage for a cup of tea before I completed the last stretch to Geitar Stadir. As we went in the door I looked out towards the South and the high cliffs.

"Jane, look. " I said, pointing. "The sun has melted nearly all the snow on the cliff walk. I would love to do that tomorrow. That was a very pleasant walk today, but that looks more of a challenge. Neither

Robert nor William expect to be back before the afternoon, so we will have time on our hands. But perhaps you have other plans. Don't let me upset them."

"No not at all. I would love to do that," she replied. "The view is magnificent from up there and the chances are there will be porpoises or whales down below. It seems to be a favourite spot for them ."

The parson had not returned from his round of visits but his wife, who Jane introduced as Sigrid entertained us. She was Danish. Small, plumpish and with a penetrating look as if she was trying to read your inner soul or maybe, I wondered if her eyesight was failing. She more or less ordered us to sit down and start eating all the goodies laid out in front of us. She had seen us coming from a long distance away and so had had the table all set and the kettle on the boil. Pastries and large sweet cakes alongside a bowl of whipped cream, all set on fine bone china, covered the beautifully embroidered tablecloth. It made me feel a little homesick and I said so. Sigrid beamed in gratitude and disappeared into her kitchen. This was a fine room with paintings of Icelandic poets and artists. The furniture was the finest I had seen in Iceland. It transpired that much of it was a wedding present from Sigrids Danish parents. There was also a grand piano. This room, Jane said, was where people would come with their problems. Be it to arrange a christening, marriage or funeral or to just ask for guidance or comfort. Also it was the meeting room for all the choir, concerts and prayer meetings.

"Be prepared for an interrogation." said Jane . "I think, she it is who runs the parish, organises choirs, all the others activities and goodness know what else. We went to church on Sunday and she plays the organ. But being so small she can hardly reach the keyboard. After the first psalm she swivelled round and peered at the congregation. Looking to see who was not there rather than who was, I suspect. Her poor husband, has quite a hard time and he is not very strong, health-wise. For all that she has a heart of gold. Here she comes." Raising her voice Jane looked at Sigrid. "How do you manage to make such a spread, alongside all your other good works?" she asks.

"I think the manse, as the Scots call it, should be a place where people want to come." said Sigrid. "If they have a problem, material or spiritual, my husband Thomas, finds there is nothing better than a little drink to give them courage to open their soul. Often they will have come a long way, so it is only right that they should leave with a full belly. Some of these people are half starving at the end of the winter. So what is the church if we cannot share our food? We hope to build a grand new church here in Husavik and the people must be behind it. I love baking and by sending out little gifts of food to the poor and needy they appreciate that the church is not just a building to go along to on a Sunday morning."

"It must be a huge project for such a small community," I said. "How do you raise the funds?

" By subscription." replied Sigrid. "We have made a start and considering the bad winters which we have had we are very hopeful that we can start building. That is in spite of the increase in prices that they are getting from your husband, Mrs Slimon. We are really appreciative of the good works that he and Mr Kogill are achieving. I have to say you have shown up my fellow countrymen, who it has to be said have in many cases exploited these good people. Not only do good prices and fair treatment help them materially but that in turn helps them spiritually. They have become so much more positive." There came a sound of a door being closed. "Ah, if I am not mistaken here comes Thomas. He will be needing his tea"

"No, no." said a voice as the door opened, "I have had enough coffee for a week. Ah, Jane, this must be Mrs Slimon. How do you do? I am Thomas." He said shaking my hand. He was a tall, slim man, slightly frail looking with thick black hair and a pleasant smile. "I have heard all about you and your husband. Have you had a good walk? What a change from yesterday."

"Yes, we have had a most pleasant walk." I said. " and as our menfolk wont be returning until late tomorrow Jane and I thought we might go up the cliff walk now that the snow is receding."

"I am told that there are a big number of whales have come into the fjord after the storm, so they could well be there tomorrow." said Thomas, pulling in a chair. "The folk were certainly hoping so as they are planning to do a bit of 'fishing' tomorrow. They are struggling to get numbers, however, as so many men are away to the reiter. But the cliff top is the best place to view as that is where the whales seem to congregate. Personally, I have never witnessed this event. I find it hard to see these magnificent beasts killed but at the same time they have been an extremely valuable source for our people. I am certain it is God's will."

" I am not sure how I shall feel" I said. "But I think it must be an extremely dangerous job and yes, I think I will regret it if I don't take the opportunity. It is not like the Spanish and their bullfights. This is for survival not sport."

"Well, I believe they intend going out at first light so you will need to leave early." said Thomas.

"Why do you not stay here for the night, Mrs Slimon?" said Sigrid. "We are so much nearer here. We will get a message to Gretel that you are staying for the night." I felt it was more of a command.

"Well that is most kind of you," I said, " I have to say that I find conversing with Gretel difficult. It is fine when John Coghill or William are there, but Gretel's English is not much better than my Icelandic. But are you sure you can manage. I don't want to put you to any bother.'

"No trouble at all," said Sigrid "When they built a parsonage they knew that the minister would be expected to use his house as a hostel. My girl will make up a bed for you and it is fish pie for supper followed by fresh berries that you picked today and cream. Now, I shall go and arrange for a message to be sent to Gretel"

"Thank you so much, Sigrid," I said. "The cream will be from that beautiful cow at the gate I noticed waiting to be milked."

"Yes, indeed," she replied, "We were given four cows and twenty sheep when we took over the charge. Some ministers don't get so many, it depends on the size of the community and the land. We are fortunate. with both the land and a very supportive congregation. Now I really must go."

"Thank you, my dear. I just love your fish pie," said Thomas. "In the meantime perhaps you might like to join me with a small sherry, Mrs Slimon. I was visiting a family today with several children, who were excited about seeing the whales being slaughtered. I sometimes find it hard as a Christian to justify the killing of such magnificent beasts." Thomas handed me a very generous sherry.

"I understand that parsons are responsible for the children's education," I said. "You must be a busy man."

"I see myself more as a Director of Education. We have a school now. It starts on the first of October and finishes on the first of April. They spend half the year helping their parents with all the farm-work. By the time the school opens again they have forgotten half of what they learnt the previous year. I try to encourage the parents to get their children to read books at night or in bad weather. Most do, and are keen for their children to go on to further education be it in Copenhagen or the colleges which are now starting here in Iceland. "

"What subjects do they learn," I asked.

"Danish and English, arithmetic, orthography, geography, history, mathematics but no arts or science, which is disappointing," replied Thomas. "But when I think how far we have come in the last decade or so, I should praise the Lord. How much better educated the children of today are. Just as essential to their education though is the life they have here, working on the land and the sea, learning how to respect nature and the weather, learning about and respecting our wonderful flora and fauna. So many are keen to move to the towns, but when I see the families that have moved to Reykjavik, the children may have parents who are materially better off but their quality of life is not."

"That will be world wide over the last century." I said. "Some of the conditions in our big cities are quite deplorable. The exploitation of children in the workhouses is terrible. But look, you must be wanting to change after your long day. Here comes Jane."The evening was spent most pleasantly with Sigrid giving a piano recital and Jane occasionally accompanying her with song. Thomas sat in his chair beside the fire with a whisky, occasionally nodding off.

The morrow broke with a blue sky but cloud was coming in from the West and rain was threatening when we left the parsonage. This encouraged us to press on and not pause too long to admire the ever expanding horizon out towards the mouth of the fjord. As we climbed the wind increased and by the time we reached the summit it was near gale force. The white horses far below were getting ever bigger and as we took shelter behind a rock to enjoy our repast, the rain started.

"What a pity," said Jane. "It is such a great view on a good day. The whalers will have had to call off too."

"And I wouldn't like to be gathering the sheep over in these hills," I said "This gale will be right in their faces and it must be nearly snow. Our menfolk can't be enjoying it either. At least, Robert and John will have this wind behind them. Maybe they will arrive a bit quicker so perhaps we should push on. It is not much fun sitting here."

There were two horses tethered outside the parsonage when we arrived back some two hours later. Jane recognising one piebald horse as that belonging to her husband.

"I hope this does not mean that the silver had gone." said Jane. "William would be able to travel so much quicker without it."

The same thought was going through my mind, when the door was flung open and there stood William with a big grin on his face.

"Welcome home both. You must be ready for a bath. Sigrid is already organising it." said William as he helped us off with our cloaks.

"I take it from your cheery countenance that your mission was successful." suggested Jane, sitting down on a chair to remove her boots.

"Indeed it was," replied William. "Stephen was sure that there was another storm coming, so we pressed on leaving our horses at a farm halfway to the silver and borrowed the farmer's horse. After a good feed we resumed the journey. Stephen recognised the spot and the snow was no deeper than when he had left it. He carried on to Reykjavik and I returned. I stopped for another meal, and a short sleep of maybe a couple of hours and got back here just as the rain started, having dropped off the silver at Geiter Stadir. Sigrid gave me a big breakfast and I have had a good sleep since. So now you go and get into the bath and get dry clothes on."

What a luxury a deep hot bath is when one is soaked and cold. Just to lie back and luxuriate for five minutes is so good for mind and body. As I lay there, though, I thought of all the poor Icelanders who came into their cold shacks, because that was what many of them were, to dry their clothes over a pitiful flame and go to bed wet, cold and, yes, often hungry especially in the springtime when the beasts were thin and dying and the cows' milk had dried up. I started thinking of that poor family at Godfoss and how would they be faring at this very moment. The bath seemed to lose all its attraction and its heat and I got out and dried myself in a mood of guilt and anger. What an ill divided world we lived in. There was I half an hour ago feeling sorry for myself because I had been caught in a shower of rain, whilst the Godfoss family were probably even now sitting shivering in the half dark, wondering if they could afford to spare the food for their evening meal.

The familiar voices of Robert and John brought me out of my gloom and hurriedly dressing, I went through to greet their arrival. They too were soaked, but having cast off their coats they were perched on either side of the roaring fire with a big glass of whisky. They rose as I came in and I suggested they should change into dry clothes before any thing else.

"As long as you are warm in the inside," said John, nodding towards his glass. " The outside will look after itself.'They had had a good trip with every thing going to plan. They were both pleased with the *Miaca*. She had performed much better than expected and she had proved to be very efficient on fuel, which was always a worry with long distances between fuel depots. The crew were a cheery lot. The Captain, whose first command it was, hailed from Old Kilpatrick on the Clyde, was an extremely good seaman and handled the boat well in the stormy seas like a veteran. He also had an never-ending repertoire of stories and whisky which helped pass the time most pleasantly. The first mate was a young Icelander who had been brought up on fishing boats and was being trained up to take over command.

Once the trading season was over the *Miaca* was to be employed as a ferry running between Iceland and Norway. Over the years Robert had established trading links with Norway, importing sheep but not anywhere in as big numbers as Iceland. There being other traders and a shorter route, the competition with the English markets was fiercer. Timber was one of Iceland's greatest needs and Norway had it in abundance. With Iceland's growing prosperity, there was an increasing demand for building. Houses, industrial buildings and offices. So timber was in big demand.

"You will experience the *Miaca* tomorrow,my dear, as we are going back round to Eskyafjord with some of Gardur and his neighbours sheep," said Robert. "The *Camoens* is due in three days time. I just hope the stormy weather has not delayed her." Turning to Sigrid, he said, "So I think if you will excuse us. We have an early start tomorrow. I am most grateful for your hospitality and for looking after Robina so well."

We said our farewells to William and Jane, promising to keep in touch. I thanked Sigrid for her splendid hospitality and headed back to Geiter Stadir.

A cloudless sky and a keen frost met us the next morning as we bade our farewells to Gretel and her family. Gardur was already at the Husavik

Eider Duck Nests on Vigur Island. They return to the same nest every year, making it easy for the farmer to collect the down. Photo by the author.

Loading Sheep on Vigur Island. Photo with permission of Salvur Olafur Baldarsson.

Note Viking lines of boat. Photo with permission of Salvur Olafur Baldarsson.

pier when we arrived. His and his neighbours sheep were loaded on the *Miaca* and they were gathered round a bench smoking their pipes or chewing tobacco, along with John Coghill, who had helped gather the sheep to the pier. There was a glass sitting on the bench and a tell tale neck of a bottle protruding from John's pocket. He had already valued the sheep, a task I had yet to witness.

"Ah, the early bird catches the worm," said John after I expressed disappointment at being too late. "You'll get your chance at Grenivik. That will be a big day. I shall have Petur to assist me, I hope. He is making his way to Grenivik from Akureyri today." I had heard of Petur. Not only were John and he both highly respected in the livestock world, but there were many tales of their exploits together.

It was a beautiful sail out of Skjalfandi with blue sky, snow topped mountains and a flat sea. A lunch of freshly made pancakes and a pot of tea in the entertaining company of our Clydeside captain made the journey even more pleasurable. Although the crew were largely Icelandic and therefore coffee drinkers, the good Captain had insisted that the option of tea be served and I thanked him for it. I had almost given up on drinking a good cup of tea till we returned to Scotland or at least the *Camoens*. It will be one of my lasting impressions of this fascinating country, their obsession with coffee. From the wealthiest to the poorest, they took pride in being able to serve a good cup of coffee. Not only the quality but also the quantity. Whether after a good days work or after a miserable day when things were going wrong , the cry was always, "lets have cup of coffee'. With the autumn sun slowly creeping up in the sky and giving a warmth after the cold of the quayside, it was hard to believe that we were within throwing distance of the Arctic Circle. Then we were heading South east into what is the longest Fjord in Iceland, Eskifjordur with Akureyri at its southern end in a much more sheltered position than Reykjavik. We were headed for an estuary about thirty miles ahead on the Eastern side of the fjord, about half way to Akureyri.

I was standing in the bow as the *Miaca* entered the mouth of the river. There was too much silt to get near to the shore. Captain McNair dropped anchor and a boat full of sheep, appeared being rowed out from the shore. We were disembarking but the *Miaca* was making for Akureyri where the *Camoens* was due in a few days time and the Miaca was taking some sheep that were too fat to walk the distance.

The farmer wanted a premium and they would lose condition on the walk he thought. They were park sheep rather than hardy hill sheep that were being gathered off the hills above us. The sheep were hoisted up in a box-like contraption eight at a time and we returned on the empty boat. Whilst a few men and a beautiful Icelandic dog loaded the boat again, a young lady came cantering down to join us. Just as she dismounted a sheep made a bid for freedom and the girl had a hold of him in a flash. It was a heavy sheep but she had it in the boat with the rest in one movement.

She turned to me, "You will be Mrs Slimon? My boss spotted the *Miaca* sailing up the fjord and sent me to meet you, I am Julianne," She said holding out her hand. Julianne turned out to be a young German lady with a string of horses. She was an enterprising young lass,who had ponies on her farm in her own country and was fascinated by the Icelandic breed. Not only ponies, but the whole Icelandic way of life. Their survival for a thousand years against climate and natural disasters. Her English was, of course, excellent as was her Icelandic. She rode beside me to the farm whilst the menfolk loaded the sheep. We passed the rett or sheepfold which, would be the centre of the community on the morrow when the gather ended here and everyone from miles around would come to sort out their sheep. They would sell their wethers to John and drive all the rest home to the various farms and crofts along the side of the fjord.

As we were tying up the horses, the lady of the house emerged with a big cake full of raisins and a pot of coffee. Raisins are one of the few Icelandic luxuries, so as guests it was much appreciated. Mugs had been set out on an upturned box at the end of the house, where a bench ran along the wall. A bottle of Schnapps appeared and glasses filled. Toasts were made to a successful reiter. Julianne, the young German girl, then took me on a tour of the farm buildings, introducing me to all the farm animals from dogs and hens to horses and cows. I got an account of virtually every beast and its pedigree. We were just finishing our tour when the clip clop of horse hooves made us look to the road below just as a man on horseback turned his steed towards the farm

" Ah, here comes Petur" said Julianne, " John will be pleased."

"Yes. So will Robert . He has a great respect for him." I added. "I have not met him yet so would be pleased if you could introduce me."

"Ah. Juliane, How are you? You look well." exclaimed Petur jumping off his horse. Petur was a big man well over six feet and broad with a big bushy beard , big eyes and when he doffed his woollen hat it exposed thick locks of almost ginger hair. Petur's father was the Goldsmith in Borg and had been John's travelling companion and translator ever since John's first sailing to Iceland back in 1870

"I am very well, thank you. It is good to see you" said Juliane. "I should like you to meet Mrs Slimon, who has just arrived with her husband and John."

" Hullo, Mrs Slimon how are you and how is Mr Slimon?"said Petur pumping my hand up and down.

"Oh! He is very well, thank you." I replied. "He is looking forward to meeting you, as is John. You must be weary, you have had a long journey." We moved round to the side of the house after Petur had tethered his horse.

John appeared having heard his friends voice. "Ah, Petur you old devil." they threw their arms round each other and slapped each other on the back like a pair of schoolboys. Robert appeared and Petur' s greeting, whilst affectionate, was much more respectful.

While the menfolk sat down with their drams, coffee and pipes, I excused myself to unpack our cases. Our room was directly above and with the window open their voices drifted up accompanied by the not unpleasant aroma of tobacco smoke. They were discussing the forthcoming marketing of the sheep,the prices they would have to pay, how to get the sheep to Akureyri, the pasture there and the rental of it and other details of the complex procedure. Petur had come via Akureyri and had all the arrangements in place They started to reminisce on exploits of previous years and Petur's booming voice and laugh became louder as the whisky took affect. I gently closed the window and lay down on the bed and closed my eyes.

"Sorry to disturb you, dear. I left these two worthies recounting past exploits. There is a very pleasant fishy aroma coming from the kitchen so perhaps we should join our hosts."

A beautifully set out table with white linen tablecloth and polished cutlery awaited us in the dining room. Tasteful furniture with pictures of German castles and meadow scenes around the sky-blue walls. A big pot of poached fish was brought in and served with bread and cabbage.

Very tasteful it was. Freshly picked berries with cream followed before the pot of coffee and sweet biscuits. All the while Petur regaled us with stories of Iceland past and present. I think he was proud of his grasp of the English language and thrilled to have a captive audience. Julianne kept translating for our hosts, who managed to follow most of the conversation but when Petur came to the climax of the story, he tended to raise his voice and run the words together.

One that he enjoyed telling was when he and John at the end of a successful days trading and after a few too many drinks had a discussion as to whose horse was the fastest. There was only one way to prove it. They would race to the next township where they were trading the next day. John was quite sure he had the fastest horse and let Petur go first whilst he settled up with the innkeeper. Petur recalled passing a shepherd, who he put in a state of alarm as he scattered the sheep he was driving along the track and shouting to him that the devil was after him. So what he thought when John appeared he could only imagine.

Petur took out his pipe as Julianne brought in the coffee. I think she sensed that I was not at my ease as she suggested that I accompany her what she called her 'bedding'. Just making sure all her beasts were happy for the night.

The sun was setting across the fjord, as I opened the door and was hit by the cold.

"It is going to be frosty tonight," I declared.

"Yes," replied Julianne. "But it will be a great day for the retter. These horses don't mind the frost, do you?" as she gave a wee treat to a nose poking over a gate. " You'll be up for the trek tomorrow, wont you?"

"I am looking forward to it but I hope I will not get in the way." I said.

'"Nonsense, there are a lot of folk turn up just for the occasion and it is all good fun."

We made our way back in the gloaming and I was glad I had my Inverness cape as the temperature was dropping rapidly.

CHAPTER 11

THE GATHER

I was awoken by the sun streaming in our east facing window or was it the cold seeping into the bedroom? A cloudless sky and the ground covered with hoar frost made a very wintry scene.

Various cold meats, bread and coffee were laid out on a side table. Robert and John came in to join me. They were going to spend the day in what we would call the sheepfold or fank but in Iceland it was a rett. Small farmers would bring their sheep and have them valued by John and Petur and they would then be walked to a holding field towards Akureyri, before the big gather or retter arrived in the afternoon.

I was going out with Julianne to meet the sheep coming in. It was bitterly cold when we went to our horses which had already been saddled up.

"Twelve degrees," Julianne answered when I asked her how cold it was. "Very cold for this time of year. It will have killed off all the berries. I had hoped to have a last picking, but not now. However, it will be warm by the time we meet the shepherds. One horse was laden with their and our mid-day meal.

Soon we were on our way. About ten of us. The farmer, out in front with two of his family, one a boy no more than eight was in charge of the Icelandic dog. We followed a steep path up a grassy slope, which led on to a scrubby stretch of ground above the river. The hill rose steeply on our right, with the snow-line not very far above.

We stopped at a traditional Icelandic house. Julianne explained that an old couple lived here and that they always stopped for coffee when they were passing. She would go in first to see how they were. I turned in my saddle to view the panorama. And what a panorama it was. The green fields and the blue and red roofed farms below stretched away to

Grenivik in the distance to the right. Across the blue fjord the sun was shining dazzlingly on the snow covered mountains

Julianne asked the others to continue and beckoned me to come in. I had to bend low and found myself in a dark passage. It took a minute or two for my eyes to adjust from the bright sunlight. Julianne took my hand along a passage and into a room at the end of which was a small fire. I could make out the form of an old man sat crouched over the embers with a long pipe in his mouth. There was a stale smell of tobacco but there was another smell even more unpleasant which made me put my spare hand to my nose. Then I almost screamed as I felt a hand grasp my leg. It was then I realised there was a body on a long bed stretched along one side of the room, which also acted as a bench. A gnarled old face was looking up at me. She was covered in what could only be described as rags. I realised that this was where the smell was emanating from.

Julianne suggested I sat on the other side of the fire by the old man, whilst she would brew a jug of coffee. I thought I was going to be sick with the stench. Julianne was explaining who I was to the old man. He turned and gave a toothless grin and then said something to Julianne in Icelandic which she translated as being that he was grateful to my husband for being able to give his son and family a chance of a new life in Canada. Julianne explained that for two long winters the family had been on the brink of starvation. But with the little cash they had been paid for their stock, both sheep and horses, they were able to pay their passage to Canada. Twenty years ago that would not have been an option. In one of the years Robert had taken ship-loads of hay at no profit to himself to the North coast where the crisis was greatest, with the ice lasting well into the summer. This action, perhaps more than any other had enhanced Roberts' reputation in Iceland.

The old woman had pulled herself into a sitting position. She took the mug of coffee in her bird like fingers, her long straggly hair falling into the mug. The flicker of the fire made her appearance even more witch like. Julianne handed her a bit of bread, which she dipped in her coffee and proceeded to chew with her gums. Julianne was reporting on the progress of the gather and obviously our visit had perked them up. Thankfully Julianne got up and made her farewells to the obvious disappointment of the old couple. She hugged them both.

"I promised I would stay longer next week." said Julianne, as we emerged blinking into the sunlight. "I don't know if they'll survive another winter up here. That's the sad bit about emigration. It is often the weak and infirm who are left behind and they can't cope with life let alone look after themselves. In some places the whole community is in danger of collapse. I come up every week and their nephew comes up at weekends when he can and cleans the place up a bit. The old man used to trek away over these hills in the summer to prevent the sheep wandering too far and then at this time of year going out after the retter to gather in the strays before winter set in "

We had mounted our horses and swung up on to the track.

"I have to say, I am full of admiration at your commitment to your neighbours," I said. "I would find it hard to re-enter that house. The smell was just overpowering."

"I know, she was much worse today and I really worry as to what to do about her. But, come on, lets enjoy the day. Lets catch up on the others"

With that she kicked her heels into the horse's withers and galloped off along the track. I did not attempt to keep up but wondered if in fact that the condition of the old lady had shocked her and to hide it she wanted to get back to the work of the day. In the normal way of life the young family would have been in the house looking after the old folk. They would not have been fit to face the long journey to Canada. It must have been a ghastly decision to make. I trotted along for a time tossing in my mind the horrible situation the family found themselves in. This would be replicated throughout the country and indeed in our own Highlands and Islands. I comforted myself with the picture of the face of the old man turning into a grateful smile. It was a genuine feeling of gratitude. I told myself that he simply wanted the best for his family. It would have been harder for the mother saying farewell to her loved ones, knowing that she would never see them again.

Suddenly I was aware of sheep walking along the track towards me. half a dozen, then another three or four, then about twenty. These were the first heading back to their wintering grounds. They gave the odd bleat as they went by making sure that they all stayed together. Then I noticed some wandering through the scrub. Some of them would have been on the move for the last three days and they appeared in good condition considering the storm and the long trek. I reached a rise that gave me a view away up the valley or glen. I could see the track for, perhaps, a mile wandering upwards along the side of the hill. The scrub was only sparse now and there looked to be better grazing. The valley narrowed and there looked to be a steady stream of sheep coming along below the snow line. Perhaps two hundred yards in front of me our party were grouped by the stream. A column of smoke rising from their midst indicated the coffee was being brewed for the shepherds. One of the party must have spotted me because he or she started waving wildly and I responded. But I tarried a while taking in this view. Not for the first time I wished I was an artist so that I could record this scene. With the cloudless sky, the snow like icing sugar having been poured over the mountains and below me the column of sheep wandering along the valley bottom with its glistening stream and setting it all off, the group of people round a campfire. As I looked down towards them a golden plover moved in little runs across the scrub in front of me. I was just about to move off when a shout, away in the distance, made me look up and I spotted a couple of horses appearing in the distance walking behind the sheep. I waited as more riders appeared on both sides of the stream and one or two away up the hill almost into the snow. There was a real heat in the sun now and I could have stayed much longer just soaking in the scene, but suddenly my appetite was on edge and I wandered down to the others,

"Come on, Mrs Slimon, we will have the first brew before the men reach us," said Julianne. "Then we can go and keep the sheep on the move."

Big mugs of coffee were being passed round along with hunks of bread and mutton. The horses were grazing down by the stream. The fire was being kept stoked by the children, who were running back and fore to a little copse, where there was some dead wood.

The flow of sheep on the track above us was getting thicker and now we could see the shepherds manoeuvring the sheep. I had assumed they would do this with their dogs, but in fact there were only two or three and the manoeuvring was done by the horses turning them when they threatened to go off the track or try dodge to higher ground. This was accompanied by shouts and whistles.

When they drew level with us they made over to the fire and dismounted. There was much shaking of hands and hugging for this was an annual ritual. For many of the shepherds this was the only time that they would come to this side of the hill. Julianne handed a bottle of whisky to the King or Fell-king as I had heard him called. The whisky was provided by John Coghill and was obviously much appreciated. Julianne came behind with mugs of coffee with the youngsters following her with plates of mutton and bread.

After every one had been provided for, Julianne shouted something in Icelandic, to which all her party immediately responded by going and mounting their horses and moving off to keep the sheep on the move and prevent them from wandering. Capable though these riders were it was immediately apparent how skilful the shepherds had been. But also the shepherds horses would be the best and much used to this kind of work. I did not attempt to leave the track but kept behind the main flock, encouraging them along, as Julianne instructed. They had to be given time. After all, many had come a great distance.

After half an hour or so, the shepherds caught up with us and Julianne returned to the track and rode alongside an old shepherd who looked extremely agile for all his advanced years. She was obviously asking him how the retter had been. Eventually she turned to me and explained that the shepherd had been on every retter for the last sixty seven years but had never experienced weather such as they had this time. Heavy snow well down the hill resulted them leaving a big number. They had to resort to lifting them out of the snow on to a track that the horses had made. I asked what would happen to the ones that had been left, to which Julianne replied that they always went back after a fortnight to gather any that had been left. This time, however, there would be a lot more than normal and they might have trouble with the weaker ones. The old man started to speak to Julianne again he was pointing and smiling at me as he spoke. When he had finished Julienne turned to me to say that thanks to the money paid by Horse Kogill his grand children were at the University of Copenhagen. One studying medicine and the other languages to become a teacher back in Iceland. This was all due to the money that Robert had introduced to the system and also because of the better prices that he and John Coghill were paying. Just speaking

Abandoned Homestead. Photo by the author.

The Autumn Sheep Roundup. The gather could take up to a fortnight'. Olafur Magnusson. Source. Akureyri Folk Museum

Sheepfold. With permission of the Reykjavik Photographic Museum.

,Sheepfold. This is the traditional design. With permission from the Icelandic Livestock. Olafur Dyrmundsson.

to his younger colleagues over the past two days made him realise how different their attitude was to the retter when he was young. Now they were talking of building new houses, buying bigger boats and travelling to Europe. In his young days, it was enough to repair the house and the boat and if they managed to the Althing they were happy.

I asked Julianne to express my thanks for his kind words and mentioned that though Robert and John had done very well out of Iceland financially, it had only been done with much hard work and many risks. The real reward was in seeing the Icelanders grow in confidence and that they could build a better country for themselves.

We were coming in sight of the fjord and more people, some on horseback some walking, were coming out to join us. The valley had widened out and the scrub was more dense. The sheep were drifting amongst the bushes, so it required more people to keep them all moving. There was now another column of sheep going along the valley bottom with yet another on the far side. Julianne informed me that there were another two coming at right angles to us along the hillside from either direction. They would be arriving ahead of us and John, Petur and his squad would be taking the wethers they wanted and settling on a price.

The old couples house was down below us now and we could see the old man standing at the door with his stick, talking to a couple of shepherds. Julianne waved and I followed suit.

" I think I'll go down and speak to him," Julianne said. "You carry on, I'll catch up."

We were now descending steeply and suddenly the rett came in view. There was great activity. The rett appeared to be full, not just with sheep but also with people. Perhaps fifty horses were tethered along a wooden paling and there was a throng of people on one side, from whence a column of smoke was rising indicating more coffee was brewing,

Julianne had caught us up. "This is where it can get difficult,"she said. "We'll have to hold them against the roadside fence, till there is room in the rett. You are lucky it is a beautiful day to just sit and wait. It is not always like this."

There was perhaps about three hundred yards of fence, along which the sheep were either standing chewing their cud or taking the chance to lie down,

Word had come back that we would have to wait about twenty minutes before we could get our lot in. Julianne took the opportunity to quiz me about my life in Scotland. I realised how different was noisy ,dirty, smelly Leith, with all its poverty and crime of every sort compared to the scene and the people in front of me. But at the same time, Leith had tremendous community spirit and, in fact, had had a school for several centuries and was not Edinburgh at the forefront of medicine and science not to mention the arts and drew students from all over the world.

"Oh, here we go, they are letting the wedders out." said Julianne. Several hundred sheep were heading down the road away from the rett, men were riding in front and behind. "They are putting them into our field for the night," said Julianne. As she said it, the sheep turned into a field below the farm. "We'll not be long now."

The men returned and opened the gate to let our sheep across the road and into the rett. It was a minute or two before they could be persuaded to cross and then just as they were beginning to flow, a dog appeared in the wrong place and they all turned back and started racing in all directions. We were half way up the steep slope and they started running past me on both sides. The horses sprang into action, their riders dashing along the sixty degree slope as if they were on the flat. They headed the sheep and turned in one quick action and headed up to turn the next lot. The eighty two year old sprang on to his horse, which was fifteen years old, and sped along the face. The 'King', his locks flowing behind came racing in the opposite direction. Soon the sheep were headed back towards the gate and never stopped running till they were in the safe confines of the rett.[1]

The rett was a like a large wheel with twelve spokes. But instead of the spokes going to the centre, they were bisected by another circular wall. The area between the spokes were the pens and each pen had a gate into the inner circle. The stone walls were about five to six feet in height. It was this inner circle where all our sheep were now, The shepherds tied their steeds to the wooden paling.

We had seen similar Sheep-folds throughout Iceland, some rougher than others. There was more than one constructed in the middle of the

---

[1] Appendix 5. Sheep weights.

lava flow of extinct volcanoes. How they got the sheep through the boulders was a mystery.

Soon the central pen was full of people of all ages catching sheep by their horns, checking their lug marks to make sure that they were the owners and then pulling them to their own pen. One of the older members of the family manned the gate checking the sheep as they were passed in. Within the pen there was a partition where any 3 year old or older wedders were placed. John and Petur were in one pen. John felt the top of the back for fat cover and the thickness of the tail. He indicated whether it was heavy enough, that is over one hundred pounds. John had a great reputation of being able to judge the weight to within one or two pounds. If it was border-line there was a balance which could be used to check. But it was slow and cumbersome. Robert applied a spot of paint to the same part of every sheep, so that when they arrived in Akureyri they could be weighed on a weigh-bridge. Some of the farmers let John judge the weights and trusted his judgement. These were generally the smaller farmers with fifty to a hundred to sell.

When they finished one pen they moved to the next. Petur kept a continual banter going and John seemed to cause continual laughter, whist Robert, diligently, kept a tally of the sheep in each pen, what their mark was and the name of the owner.

This year demand was high and there was no dispute over the price paid. Two years ago it was the same but last year there had been a drought in Britain and there were no crops to fatten the sheep. Prices had dropped dramatically and Robert and John had lost money. So also had some Iceland dealers, who thought they could capitalise on this trade. They had bought wedders in the spring time, hoping to make a profit by the autumn but had lost out on their initiative.

Whilst the work was going on Julianne suggested we get some sustenance. There was a big throng around a canvas tent, mostly youngsters who had got tired of their exertions dragging sheep. Some of the older ladies had a big pot simmering on a converted oil drum. A sort of broth soup smelt delicious, coffee and cold mutton was followed by slabs of fruit cake. This was a great community occasion. All ages joined together, working together for the good of the community. There was much banter and hugging of friends who perhaps had not seen one another since the same occasion the previous year. All the while the work continued in the rett. When we had got our soup, we returned to the slope overlooking the rett. The central pen was almost empty. John Robert and Petur were well round the circle and there seemed to be good chat going on. I gathered that the sheep in spite of the atrocious weather at the beginning of the week were in very good condition and a record number of wedders were over the obligatory one hundred pound weight.

"There will be a few drinks poured tonight," said Julianne. "It is as well we live close by. Some of them have several miles to go with their flocks and they'll not get there before dark. It is lucky that it is a clear sky and will be almost a full moon. Look, I think your husband wants you."

Robert was waving to me to go over to the pen which was the last to be sorted. He gave me his note book in which he had been entering the total wedders marked in each pen. One by one the wedders were counted again as a check in each pen and then let out into the big circular pen. Robert was very good at counting. He counted in fours as they ran past into the big pen, then called out the total which I checked against the number he had entered. At the end each pen had been counted three or four times and there was only one pen where Roberts figure was disputed and, in fact, it was in the farmer's favour.

I am not a judge of sheep, but when I saw all the wedders in the big ring, they looked very impressive. John had said they were in the best condition he had seen and with a promise of a good price the farmers were all in a good mood. The gate was being opened and off they charged, several hundred, some of them kicking their heels in the air as they thought to escape. But this was just the start of a long trip to Scotland and then a winter fattening up on fields of parsnips. They were joining the others in Julianne's field, or rather her boss's, and the day after tomorrow they would start walking to Akureyri. The *Camoens* was due in four days time. I was having mixed feelings about leaving this extraordinary country. I could well understand how everyone who experienced it seemed to come under its spell.

The action now moved to the track outside where a pony had arrived with gold and silver. Robert knew the number that each farmer was selling. John and Petur had estimated their average weight, generally about a hundred and ten pounds, but in addition there were two pens of sheep which John was particularly complimentary about and was prepared to pay a premium on. This he hoped would encourage others to improve their stock by paying more for the best tups or rams. When the sheep got to Akureyri they would be sorted in their respective lots and as they went on to the boat, they were passed over a weigh-bridge twenty or so at a time. That would be the proper check and any balance deducted or added to next years total. One by one Robert called out the names. As they came forward John checked the figures. It was not simply a case of paying them for their sheep. Most had bought supplies in the Spring on credit. This was subtracted from their sheep total. As John checked out the figures, the farmer was asked to check also. I counted out the money, the farmer checked it and Robert gave him a little bag to put it in. As we were paying out to the last farmer, three or four shepherds and numerous children moved off behind the sheep, that were going to the furthest farm. I turned back to the rett. Drams were being poured by John to all the farmers and any others who would partake.

There seemed to be a discussion going on about one particular animal, a big ram.

"That is what we call a 'Leader'." explained Julianne. "They are bred especially for leading the sheep into the mountains. They are very muscular and are kept purely for their 'leader' qualities and fetch high prices. There is no other sheep breed have them."

"That's very interesting," I said. "I had noticed one or two when we were on the hill but had not appreciated that they were special."

It had been a long day, and now the sun was falling behind the distant hills . The sky to the east was a red glow reflecting off the snow. The men were enjoying their broth and mutton before moving off.

"They take it turns to take their sheep out," said Julianne, moving to the side of the track as a pen of sheep was being let out into the big pen prior to their being set off on the road. An old farmer was being helped on his horse, obviously having had too much to drink. Two boys, the oldest of which was maybe fourteen. got on their horses ."Those that have the furthest go first. Its always the way with Olaf. He says its good for the boys to take some responsibility. It'll be dark before they get home. Now. if you don't mind I'm going back to the farm to bed down my beasts. The boss will manage our beasts. He will be the last to leave. Petur, John and your husband will help him.'

"Oh, I think I shall come too, if you don't mind." I said. " This seems a good time to go. I have really enjoyed the whole day, thank you so much for everything"

"It has been a great pleasure," replied Julianne. "Except, perhaps, for the old couple. I am sorry about that."

"Oh, don't be." I said. 'I think to come to a foreign country and start taking care of old folks is something you should be very proud of. They were obviously very fond of you."

We were turning into the farm now and I suddenly realised I was quite tired, so I excused myself. " I think I shall heat up some milk, would you like some?"

"Yes, please, that would be good." said Julianne, as she disappeared into the buildings and her beloved animals.

CHAPTER 12

AKUREYRI 3 EMBARKATION

I think for the first time on this trip I was up before my husband. In fact it was he that got me up. His snoring, always a sign that he has had a few drams, was so loud that I gave up trying to sleep and with the sun streaming in our window I thought I would arise and go for a walk before breakfast.

"Is that man of yours still sleeping?" said the familiar voice of John Coghill in the passage-way. "We are supposed to be on the road within the hour. I think he had one too many last night. The farmers were in great form and, in fact, there are two lots of sheep still in the pens."

"Oh, I had not realised that we were to be so early. I am sorry. I shall go and waken him."

When I got back to the room, Robert was up and rushing about pulling on his clothes. "Why did you not waken me? We need to get on the road. There are sheep to be bought and we are supposed to be mid-morning at Laufas. They had sheep here yesterday and they have some more to be graded. They have invited us for coffee mid-morning and I hate to be late. It is the ministers farm so it is important that we make a good impression. He did John and the farmers a good deed last year. I'll tell you about it later." I started packing my things and soon we were down in the kitchen where there were plates of porridge and skyr. We did not wait for coffee. We apologised to our hostess, who seemed quite amused by our unseemly haste.

John and Petur, the goldsmiths son, assisted by Julianne were out saddling the horses. It was only when we were en route that Robert turned to John and asked him to recount his tale from last year

John, who was riding in front, turned in his saddle, "I had a bit of trouble last year. There is a very arrogant farmer, who always demands an exorbitant price. After a time arguing, I simply rode away refusing to meet his demands. They thought I would simply return and agree. I felt sorry for the majority, who I knew were willing to accept my offer. However, the next day they arrived at Akureyri, all except Mr Arrogant and said they were happy to accept my figure. Apparently the Parson had intervened and persuaded the farmers to go and see me but without the troublemaker. I asked if they had killed him and they roared with laughter. "We thought about it" one said. Anyway, I think if you are just present, Mrs Slimon, there will be no trouble, I hope so anyway. Last year I had been late which meant the mood was not good when I arrived, so I am keen not to be late this year,"

It was a pleasant ride along the fjord, with Petur telling a never ending number of stories. Once he interrupted himself, pointing up to the sky at a gyr falcon circling above a patch of scrub. "Ah, your hawk, Mr Slimon," he called turning in his saddle. He was, of course referring to the one on the flag that Robert had been presented with. "That was a big occasion for you. I was invited and very sorry not to be able to be there."

Laufas was a manor farm with a splendid new house and what was reputed to be a very old church beside it or at least some of the interior was very old. Apparently there had been habitations here going right back to the days of the settlement. The farmers were still pulling out the wedders when we arrived. One of the older farmers came forward with a bottle and a glass and spoke to Petur, who translated saying that they were looking forward to doing business with us. A fourteen or fifteen year old girl came out of the house and asked if Mr and Mrs Slimon would care to have some coffee with Mrs Halldorsson. Robert felt he should be helping with the sheep but John insisted that he thought it diplomatic to accept the invitation. Robert did not argue and,indeed admitted he was still feeling a bit rough.

A tall dark slim lady, with a pleasant smile was standing at the door of the house.

"Welcome to our home I am afraid my husband is visiting a very ill man, he is sorry to miss you." said the lady stepping aside. " Please come in and tell me of your travels."

"Oh, certainly, we would be delighted." I said. She stood aside and we passed through the three doors into the normal long dark passage. A door to the right stood open and Mrs Halldorsson indicated we should enter. This was a bright airy room with a modern window. It had a table and chairs , a large mirror opposite the window which helped lighten the room and three photos of what I now recognised as well known Icelandic authors and poets. It struck me that where we might worship our great warriors and monarchs with pictures, the Icelanders have poets and authors .

"What a pleasant room, I like the shade of blue," I said. "We were admiring the outside walls and the turf roof. You must have very skilled builders."

"Yes, I suppose so." she replied. "It is the way the houses have been built for centuries. I see many Danish type houses in Akureyri now. I am told they are not so warm in the winter."

"I can believe that," said Robert. "It is the same in our Highlands. Some of the big clan chiefs have built grand new houses and castles. But one, Lord Lovat, uses his castle to entertain his guests but goes back to sleep in his old black-house because he found it cosier with no draughts. We have stayed in a lot of cosy houses on our travels in Iceland."

"So tell me where you have travelled. You must know Iceland much better than I." she said.

I started recounting our trip and when I mentioned Thingvellur and the Althing, she interrupted and said that she had been there a few years ago at the big celebrations of one thousand years of settlement. This she said had been the most memorable weeks of her life. Her husband had played a big part in the ceremony and since she was a very good knitter, had got high praise for her work. She was in fact wearing a beautiful black and white jersey that she had knitted herself. The young girl, who had brought in a tray with coffee and buns, now returned, saying something to her mistress.

"The men appear to be finished in the rett, but they will have their smoke, so we will have time to look at the church." said Mrs Haldorsson.

"We have noticed they like their tobacco almost as much as coffee. But, I would love to see your church," I said. "I believe the pulpit is very old."

"Yes, that is so. It is beautifully carved. We are very proud of our little church. It is full every Sunday." By this time we were walking over to the church and I could see John looking up . They were apparently ready to go and I knew he was anxious to get to Akureyri. The church was, indeed, a fine building and I showed my appreciation by putting a few krona in a bowl. Soon we were walking down to the men and I remarked how young some of them were, just boys.

The ministers wife explained that most of them stayed in her house and were kept busy fishing, milking and mucking out the ten or so cows, with the lambing, with the down to collect and then in wet days clean it. Then there was the hay. Many were orphans. The girls had plenty to do in the house with the laundry, mending and sewing. There was butter and cheese making as well as baking and cooking. At the moment there were twenty four living in the house, manor or manse. I am not sure which. But she said there had been as many as thirty. It seemed a very happy household and we were sorry not to have met the head of it. Apparently, it was his drive that had got the manor farm and church built.

As we approached John was pouring a dram, everyone seemed in good form and this year there was no dispute over the price offered. Trading conditions in Britain had improved so we were able to pay a better price.

It was late when we rode into Akureyri but our hotel was ready for us. After a hot relaxing bath, we came down to the dining room where the choice was between halibut, mutton or guillemot. I chose the latter as I had yet to taste it. I was expecting a fishy taste, but if you had blind folded me, I would have said it was liver I was eating. Very tender it was.

Robert had the halibut in milky sauce "You can't beat Icelandic fish. There must be something in the water or maybe it is the temperature. The further North you go the better the taste."

There was a pile of mail that had arrived and I left Robert to deal with it before the light faded. It was a beautiful evening looking up the fjord so I took a walk along the street and then out towards the harbour. This was the third time I had walked along here in the past few weeks and it was beginning to feel like home as I recognised various people and we nodded to each other in recognition. When I came within smelling distance of the shark factory I retraced my steps. It was nearly dark when I reached the hotel. Turning round to shut the door I was aware of a funny glow in the sky and as I watched, the glow grew into yellows and greens. I ran upstairs and burst into the room giving Robert quite a start.

"Come quickly, it's the Northern Lights." I said excitedly.

I ran back down and out of the door fearful that they would have disappeared, but they had grown and were dancing across the sky directly above us like great curtains blowing in the wind

We stood mesmerised as the other guests joined us in the street. Both Robert and I had seen them in Edinburgh, but they were on the distant northern horizon and while spectacular enough, this was altogether different. In Iceland where there is so much of contrast, volcanoes, lava and earthquakes, glaciers, snow and floods, all of which can be devastating to life on this land, it was magical to see such beauty. Mine host appeared with a tray of drinks to 'toast the angels dancing'. We stood chatting for about half an hour, then the lights began to fade and disappear. It was as if Iceland was saying that this is the grand finale, "Bon Voyage and Haste Ye Back" for tomorrow we would hopefully be back aboard the *Camoens*.

While I spent the morning buying little gifts, mostly woollen gloves and scarves for friends and relations back home, Robert, Petur and John were arranging for the arrival of the vast number of sheep that were to accompany us on our return voyage. There were some sheep to be graded as well from farms on the other side, to the west, of Akureyri.

I was heading back to the hotel, when a voice from the other side of the street, hailed me, "Mrs Slimon." I looked over and at first did not recognise Mrs Stefansson, not having seen her in her fur coat and hat before. She crossed over and insisted that I have lunch with her. Her husband was not at home and I could tell her of my travels. Her husband had been given a haunch of reindeer and if I would like to leave my purchases at my hotel and then go to her home, she would be ready. I did as I was bid, as I had planned nothing more than a last walk to the waterfall.

A beautiful linen tablecloth was covered, with plates of venison and bowls of potatoes, carrots, cabbage and turnip. The vegetables had come on the last trip of the *Camoens* .

Mrs Stefansson said. "I have been trying to grow carrots and parsnips, but they are not ready yet but are looking good. I must show them to you after you have your bowl of rhubarb and skyr. I remember you enjoyed it before you went off on your travels. You must tell me all about your trip and what you think of our country and our people."

This was the first time I had tasted reindeer and I found it not as gamey as our red deer but more so than roe-deer. There was a very tasty berry sauce to go with it, which Mrs Stefansson had made herself.

We spent a very pleasant afternoon together. I reminiscing on the wonderful trip that I had had, the scenery, the people and their way of life. Mrs Stefansson relating the life of a quickly expanding port. With the opening up of trade, there was great potential for Akureyri. It was a much better and more sheltered harbour than Reykyavik. At last, Icelanders were beginning to reap the rewards of their biggest asset, fish.

"Do you know, Mrs Slimon" said Mrs Stefansson. "That there are over two hundred words in Icelandic for parts of a cod's head? Such was our dependancy on this as our staple diet through the spring and summer that we had to get maximum value. The Danes forced us to use small open boats, they gave very little for the few fish that we managed to catch, that we had to eat the heads. Although, in fact, the head is extremely nutritious and also is good for our brains, so we are told."

"Our island folk are also very clever and they say that eating fish brains is the reason and I have been very impressed how well educated everybody in Iceland is. Scotland is well known for its good education but I think we could learn a few things from you" I said.

"We are starting to build schools and colleges. The ministers have done a fine job until now, but then the responsibility goes onto the mother. and whilst there are some great teachers amongst them they don't all have that aptitude. Now, come on and I will show you my garden. It is not very big ."

As we came out of the door, Mrs Stefansson exclaimed, "Oh, look, unless I am mistaken, thats the *Camoens*."

I looked to where she was pointing in the distance. My heart missed a beat as I saw the unmistakable lines of our ship with smoke trailing out behind.

" She is right on time. One is never quite sure. Tomorrow will be a busy day weighing and loading the sheep, so we should embark this evening."

Sheep embarking over weighbridge in Akureyri. With prmission from the Akureyri Folk Museum.

After a brief tour, I bid a fond farewell and promised to keep in touch as well as making sure she would visit our Edinburgh home, so that I could reciprocate the hospitality.

Early next morning, I was awoken by the bleating of sheep and shepherds shouting at dogs, sheep and their fellow shepherds. We were back in our old berth amidships. Robert had been up early helping John and the Captain organise the weighing and loading of their purchases.

Firstly the sheep and been sorted into their various lots by the paint marks. There was a weigh-bridge moved to the side of the ship and as they went on, Robert, with the farmer to check beside him wrote down the weight of each lot. With a deckhand to assist, Robert paid over the money due. The sheep then ran onto the ship and into pens below deck. The sheep had to be at the right density. They had to be able to lie down but if the ship hit heavy seas,the deckhands made the pens smaller so that they stood close together. This way they could not be thrown into a corner and smothered. The decks were covered with a good depth of sawdust to soak up the urine and thus prevent the sheep becoming dirty.

Once again the weights were to everyone's satisfaction, which made for happy customers. Robert's worry was that he did not have enough money to pay for the record weights, but in the end all were paid and went home content. I spent the morning getting our cabin to my liking and renewing my acquaintance with the crew. There was a new chief steward, by the name of Sandy Matheson, who hailed from the Island of Lewis. A tall good looking man in his thirties, he had a reputation for being meticulous, yet having a great sense of humour and an inexhaustible fund of stories mostly about characters of his native island.

Suddenly Robert appeared in the cabin saying we were about to cast off. We went back on deck to say our hurried farewells to John and Petur. They were going on the *Miaca* to Seydafjordur to grade more sheep for the next trip.

The Captain wanted to catch the tide and by mid-afternoon we were underway sailing down Ekjifjordur past now familiar landmarks. It was a beautiful evening, the setting sun turning the snow copper coloured. We were heading for the mouth of the fjord when we were called to our dinner. There were few passengers this time. The tourist season was past. There was an Icelandic family, who were travelling to

Canada. They seemed to have private means and were planning to go to Winnipeg. There was also a couple of young English botanists, from Cambridge University, who had had a successful summer roaming the North East of Iceland.

By the time we rose from our meal of roast beef and a bowl of fruit salad, we were sailing close to the Arctic Circle. The night was cold and Robert had had a long hard day and was happy to retire early. The students entertained me with their adventures of the past weeks and they too had been impressed with the Icelanders hospitality .

After a fast and uneventful passage we sailed into Granton at four in the morning three days later.

It was quite a sight seeing the four thousand sheep being driven along the quayside on their way to fresh pasture. Even after the long trip they still managed to kick their heels as they jumped off the ship. In a couple of days they would make their way to the Lauriston Market under the shadow of the Castle Rock. I decided to visit the market to say farewell to these beasts to which I suddenly felt attached.

So it was that two days later my adventure ended when Robert entered with two hundred wedders at a time,filling the ring. All were graded into size and fat cover. Again they looked very well. A tribute to the Icelandic flockmasters. The bidding was brisk and the buyers paid tribute to Robert on their good condition, after such a long journey. Those that weren't being slaughtered would be journeying to Fife, the Lothians and even to Lincolnshire and Yorkshire, to be fattened on fields of parsnips and turnips. Then to possibly feed some of the miners who were looking after the Icelandic pit ponies.

MAP OF ICELAND
The route by Robina Slimon on her Journey

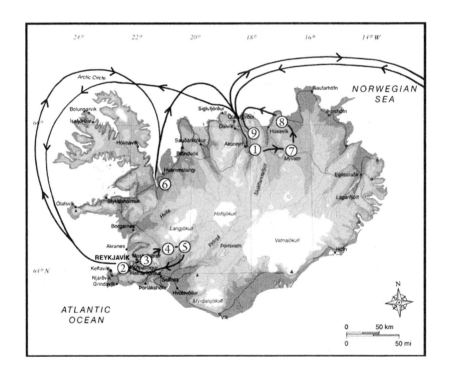

APPENDICES

APPENDIX ONE

ROBERT SLIMON

BORN 1828 DIED 5 JANUARY 1898
CARNWATH, LANARKSHIRE
WHITBURGH ESTATE,
PATHHEAD.

Robert was one of eleven children born to William, a farmer, at Carnwath in Lanarkshire in 1828. After also farming at South Gyle farm to the West of Edinburgh, we find William in 1840 as a dairyman in Gyle St, Leith.

Robert, aged 12, is employed as an ironmonger. In probably the same ironmongers, which was established in 1829, that he owned in 1859, aged 31. As well as ironmonger, the business on the '40-43 Shore' Leith, was ship chandler, plumber, tinsmith, engineers, furnishers, coppersmiths and sheet metal workers. He was also involved in export and the salvage business.

1860s Robert had the agency for importing ponies from Germany.

1865. Aged 37, marries Robina Lauder, the daughter of a local shipping agent. They had no children.

1868. Brother David comes into partnership. R. & D. Slimon. David died in 1869. The firm existed till the 1970s.

1870 Sends the first ship, John & James under Capt. John Coghill to Iceland to start the trade in horses and sheep that lasted till the 1890s. Also organised tourist treks to Geyser. Agent for the Allan Line taking emigrants to Granton for their onward journey to America.

1885. Robert along with Captain John Coghill is honoured by the Icelandic government.

1888. Robert retires to his Whitburgh Estate, Pathhead, South of Edinburgh.

1893. Robina dies.

1898. Robert dies on the 5th January.

APPENDIX TWO

Captain JOHN COGHILL

Born March 9 1837 at Weydale Mains three miles south of Thurso in the far north of Scotland. While still young the family moved to Orkney across the Pentland Firth where from an early age he herded sheep on the islands of Hoy and Shapinsay. In 1855 he goes to sea.

Spends 10 years at sea. Firstly in the Newcastle owned schooner *Non Such*. He sailed to India twice, the West Indies and the Mediterranean as well as local trade.

He stayed ashore for a year studying for his ticket in 1864. He stayed with his sister in Edinburgh, along with his mother as his father had died in 1859.

In April 1865 he took command of the Leith cutter, Britannia. He must have decided that steam was the future because we find him as an AB on the Danzig for two trips to the Baltic.

This was followed by service on Robert Slimon's schooner *Arundel Castle*. He then came ashore to take his masters ticket. It could be that Robert had encouraged him as the next thing he is in charge of the *John and James* sailing to Iceland and the start of the connection to Iceland for the rest of his days.

Initially he was trading in ponies and then a few years later sheep, which was to become a major part of the trade of R&D Slimon.

John continued to command various ships of the Slimon fleet as his trading commitments allowed.

He married Anne Rennie Parrot, a widow with seven children in 1868. They had one son, Donald (1869-1908). In Iceland he had six children to four women, four of whom immigrated to Manitoba. His wife died in 1886. He then lived with his step-daughter in Granton.

He died on 3rd October 1896 on board the *Opal* returning to Iceland where he wanted to die. He was buried at sea off the Faroe Islands.

APPENDIX THREE

Diary Summary 1860–1895

1860s Agency for importing horses and ponies from Germany.

1870 Schooner 'John & James' under Capt. John Coghill sailed for Iceland returning with fish but a second trip brought 66 ponies.
Yarrow exported 740 tons of coal returning with 302 ponies and a further 300 on a second voyage.

1871 Competition from Robert Buist. Looking at importation of sheep to extend season.

1873 Foot and Mouth in Iceland. Just two voyages by the 'Yarrow'.

1874 'Yarrow' laid up. Foot and Mouth no exports.
'Yarrow' damaged off Dunkirk in November.

1875 'Fifeshire' chartered for two voyages. Broke shaft, towed to the Faroes.

1876 'Fusilier' made four voyages, but on fifth broke prop shaft off Iceland but because of heavy weather was forced to set sail for Orkney 400 miles distant.
'Gnome' was sent to take outward cargo. First large number of emigrants, 741 & 500 in July on 'Verona' chartered.

1877 Five trips for livestock on 'Snowdoun' and 'Waverley'. same number of ponies but sheep increase by 100%.

1878 'Cumbrae' purchased for passenger and livestock under Capt. J.W. Robertson.
'Prince Alfred' sailing from Granton with the first 'package tour' when 30 tourists embarked to view the volcanic eruption of Mt Hekla.

1879 '*Camoens* bought to replace 'Cumbrae', a bigger boat. Crew of 28. First under Capt. Coghill,then Capt. Robertson. She made 6 voyages carrying 4441sheep, 1000 ponies and emigrants.

1880 5 voyages, 1389 ponies 'Verona' also made 2 voyages.

1881 After severe winter, North iced up till the end of June. 'Camoens' 6 voyages 6,000 sheep 1500 ponies. 'Cumberland' 3 voyages 4,600 sheep 575 ponies. Because of increased trade 'Craigforth' was bought. Husavik used for first time and farmers agreed to build suitable pier and trading house. Farmers form co-operative.

1882 Severe winter caused increase in exports as Iceland was short of 'keep'. 22,000 sheep 2,100 ponies. Ice still a problem 26 August.

1883 Early start. 'Camoens' returns to Granton 10 June with 219 ponies + passengers.'Camoens' ice damaged 19 June. Because of ice delays 711 emigrants arrive 10 August on 'Camoens' National flock drops 100,000 to 400,000.

1884 'Camoens' runs aground in Bruneness, Orkney, on 6 July. 'Craigforth' runs aground at Rosehearty Aberdeenshire on 18 October with 3168 sheep and 16 ponies. 600 sheep drown Capt Sutherland loses his certificate.

1886 Very good season. 22,786 sheep (including over 12,000 in 13 days from Akureyri). 1536 ponies, Purchase of 'Miaca' to be used as feeder vessel.

1887 Severe winter. Ice in Seydisfjordur in late August. Small boats put into service. 'Camoens' last year. sold to Italy.

1888 'Copeland' purchased. third voyage wrecked in fog on Stroma in Pentland Firth. with loss of 100 ponies. 120 on deck saved. 'Princess Alexandra' purchased as replacement. Trade established with Norway as Iceland trade dropping.

1889 'Magnetic' purchased. Only had 50% of trade.

1890 High number of sheep landed caused British farmers to call for restrictions on numbers imported. 35,000 down to 2,000 in 1891.

1894 14,807 sheep 37 ponies and 4 reindeer in 3 journeys in the 'Prior'

1896 John Coghill dies at sea off the Faroe Islands on his way to Iceland.

1898 Robert Slimon dies at Whitburgh, Pathead.

APPENDIX FOUR

ROBERT and DAVID SLIMON

Emigrants and Exports from Iceland 1870–1895

- Sheep 181,000 +1,500 for other agents.
- Horses 24,800 + 1,200 for other agents.
- Cattle 6 + 400 for other agents.
- Misc. Ice, 4 reindeer, 700 brace ptarmigan, 7 falcons.
- Largest number on one trip : Sheep 5534 on the Prior 28 Sept 1894.
- Horses 960 on the *Camoens* 18 Sept 1882
- Largest number in one year : Sheep 35,473 in 1890.
- Horses 2,126 in 1882.
- EMIGRANTS. Total 3130.

N.B. This figure is incomplete. For the years 1887 to 1890 there was an annual uplift in late June, with no figure recorded. The average number during this period was around 250 per trip, so we can assume that we can add 1000 to the above total. ie 4130. There were other carriers but generally it is accepted that Robert Slimon took perhaps two thirds of the total number of emigrants. The period that this took place was from 1873 to 1890. The largest number on one trip was 741 on the Verona on the 7 July 1876 and then 500 eleven days later. How such a number were accommodated on such a small vessel is not known. Slimons had an arrangement with both the Anchor and Allan Line, whereby a contract was signed by the family for a fare to the American continent via ship to Granton, train to Glasgow and passage to their destination. They were provided with hot and cold water but they had to find their own food.

APPENDIX FIVE

Weights of sheep exported to Britain from Icelandic regions in 1884 and 1885

Nöfn sveitanna, sem sauð-irnir eru úr.	Meðaltal af vigt allra sanðanna 1884	Meðaltal af vigt þeirra 1885	Meðaltal af vigtinni samanl. bæði árin	At hverjum 100 sauð-um var haustið 1885 neðan við 110 pd.	120 pd. og þar yfir.
1. Keldahverf	108,25	112,90	110,65	44,25	25,29
2. Tjörnnes	112,00	113,37	112,94	37,16	20,51
3. Reykjahverf	112,75	113,86	113,23	27,85	25,00
4. Mývatnssveit	116,15	117,71	116,95	18,90	42,26
5. Bárðardalur	116,25	119,08	117,74	8,66	50,00
6. Ljósavatnspláz	115,88	115,73	115,81	15,80	26,52
7. Kaldakinn	109,09	110,57	109,30	45,33	13,33
8. Aðaldalur og Skriðuhverf	110,83	114,94	113,05	32,90	27,74
9. Laxárdalur	114,51	113,52	113,56	35,61	29,45
0. Reykjadalur	114,21	115,06	114,65	20,83	26,39
11. Fnjóskadalur	108,37	107,97	108,17	64,06	7,82
12. Eyjafjörður	112,70	111,05	111,45	47,95	15,20
13. Höfðahverf		123,40		1,79	65,75

Skýrsla um vænleik á sauðum frá „Kaupfjelagi Þingeyinga", sem sendir voru til Englands haustin 1884 og 1885.

Húsavík í janúar 1886.
J. Hálfdánarson.

Columns description

1. Icelandic Regions
2. Average weights in 1884
3. Average weights in 1885
4. Average weights of 1884 and 1885
5. Average weights over 110 lbs
6. Average weights over 120 lbs

(1 kilo = 2.2 lbs (pounds))

APPENDIX SIX

This was written about **Robert Slimon**'s death in the Magazine Bjarki on the 5th of February 1898:

> **Gamli Slimon** er dáinn og mun reynast að Ísland hefur misst þar spón úr aski sínum sem hann var. Verslun landsins á Slimon mikið að þakka. Hann var einn aðalforkólfur hrossaverslunarinnar og fjárkaupa hans munu margir sakna. Þar var mikið af auði, þoli og áræði saman komið, sem Slimon var. Hann var að mörgu leiti sómakarl og tryggur vinur sínum.

In English it would be somehow like that:

> "Old Slimon is dead and it is clear that Iceland has lost a lot. The commerce of Iceland owes Slimon a lot. He was one of the leaders in the trade of horses and sheep and many will miss him. In Slimon there was a lot of wealth, endurance and daring. He was a good man in many ways and faithful to his friends."

APPENDIX SEVEN

OFFICIAL COPY.

(No. 3599.)

"COPELAND" (S.S.)

The Merchant Shipping Acts, 1854 to 1876.

IN the matter of a formal Investigation held at the Sheriff Court House, Edinburgh, on the 24th and 27th days of August 1888, before JOHN CAMPBELL SHAIRP, Esquire, Sheriff-substitute of Mid Lothian, assisted by Captain KENNETT HORE and Captain EDWARD BROOKS, into the circumstances attending the stranding of the steamship "COPELAND," at Stroma Island, Pentland Firth, on 25th July 1888.

Report of Court.

The Court, having carefully inquired into the circumstances attending the above-mentioned shipping casualty, finds, for the reasons stated in the annex hereto, that the stranding of the steamship "Copeland" was caused by the master having allowed too much for the set of the tide, and having accordingly altered his course to the southward, under the impression that the vessel had passed Stroma Island, whereas she was in reality still to the westward of it. Further, the master was unable to verify the distance run from Dunnet Head owing to the dense fog which prevailed and the currents which were running. The Court is of opinion that the master committed a very grave error of judgment in attempting to make the passage of the Pentland Firth in such weather, but for the reasons stated they do not deal with his certificate.

Dated this 27th day of August 1888.

(Signed)   J. C. SHAIRP, Judge.

We concur in the above report.

(Signed)   KENNETT HORE,   } Assessors.
            EDWARD BROOKS, }

Annex to the Report.

This was an inquiry into the loss of the British steamship "Copeland," held before John Campbell Shairp, Esquire, Advocate, Sheriff substitute, at the Sheriff Court House, George IV. Bridge, Edinburgh. Mr. Smith appearing for the Board of Trade, Mr. Sunderland for the master, and Mr. Kelly watched the case on the part of the owner.

The "Copeland," which forms the subject of this investigation, was an iron screw steamer of 438 tons register, and 798 gross tonnage, built in Govan in the year 1874, classed 100 A 1 at Lloyd's, and registered at the Port of Leith, her official number being 71,681. She was 225 ft. 3 in. in length, 29 ft. 3 in. in breadth, and 15 ft. 5½ in. in depth, and at the time of the casualty was owned by James Gourley Bridges, Esquire, of No. 40, Shore, Leith, who was also the managing owner. She was rigged as a three-masted schooner, and fitted with two surface-condensing compound engines of 150 horse-power combined, and had a passenger certificate from the Board of Trade to carry 566 passengers, and was engaged in the Iceland trade, running between Leith and Rigkjavik, and was also

fitted to carry cattle. She had five boats of 878 cubic feet capacity, fitted with all requisites for use when last surveyed and inspected by the Board of Trade surveyor on the 13th June 1888. She had three compasses, one on the bridge, a steering compass, and the third placed before the steering gear aft. They were all in good order and condition, and properly adjusted by Messrs. White, of Glasgow, in May 1888, who were also the makers of the compasses. The standard compass being correct magnetic on all points except six, viz. : E., E. by N., and E.N.E., S.E., S.E. by S., and S.S.E., even on these points there was only 1° of deviation. The "Copeland" was commanded by Mr. Charles Thompson, (who holds a certificate of competency as master, numbered 5,183), and had a crew of 30 hands all told, and eleven passengers when she last left Iceland. She was in every respect well found, and properly fitted and equipped for the voyage.

She left Rejkjavik on the 20th of July last with a general cargo consisting of fish, wool, and 482 ponies, bound for Leith, and her draught of water on leaving that place was 11 ft. forward and 15 ft. aft. She seems to have encountered very heavy N.E. and easterly gales after her departure, and her passage had thus been a long one up to the time of her making the land off Strathie Point. At this time the wind and sea had fallen, a dense fog had set in, with light easterly airs, and the ship's engines were put at half speed. On the morning of the 25th July, at 6 a.m., the fog lifted, and the second mate, who was then in charge of the deck, sighted, as he said, Strathie Point. A course was steered eastwards towards Dunnet Bay along the land, the vessel being stopped at times to take soundings. The master's object in taking these soundings seems to have been to make Dunnet Head, and so to get a good departure for running through the Pentland Firth. As the weather was so thick as to oblige the ship to proceed at half-speed, it seems to have been a very desirable and prudent course to take these soundings. But the Court are of opinion that, looking to the state of the weather when the "Copeland" made Dunnet Head, and knowing, as the master did, that the tides there run from 5 to 10 knots an hour, it was by no means a prudent thing to attempt the passage of the Pentland Firth in so dense a fog. How dense this fog must have been is proved by the fact that those on board the "Copeland" could not see the lighthouse on Dunnet Head when passing within half-a-mile of it; while the master states himself that when the ship struck on Stroma Island they could not see more than a ship's length a-head. To attempt the passage of the Pentland Firth under such conditions seems the more imprudent when it is remembered that the lead could have been of but very little use or the log either, when running in such a tremendous tide-way. And seeing that the principal thing required was an accurate knowledge of the distance run, and the course made good in passing through the Firth, it seems in the opinion of the Court that the best course would have been for the master to have remained in or off Scrabster Roads till the weather cleared sufficiently to make Stroma Island. Probably the ship would only have been detained a few hours by doing this. However, on making and passing Dunnet Head a fishing boat was sighted and hailed, the vessel stopped and boarded by the fisherman (or pilot as he called himself), and a telegram sent on shore to the owners. Some conversation seems to have taken place between the master and the fisherman-pilot as to the strength of the tide, the time it would

LONDON:
PRINTED FOR HER MAJESTY'S STATIONERY OFFICE,
BY EYRE AND SPOTTISWOODE,
PRINTERS TO THE QUEEN'S MOST EXCELLENT MAJESTY.

And to be purchased, either directly or through any Bookseller, from
EYRE AND SPOTTISWOODE, EAST HARDING STREET, FLEET STREET, E.C.; or
ADAM AND CHARLES BLACK, 6 NORTH BRIDGE, EDINBURGH; or
HODGES, FIGGIS, & Co., 104, GRAFTON STREET, DUBLIN.

1888.

Price Twopence.

54010—101.   375.—8/88.   Wt. 23.   E. & S.

run, and the state of the weather, and also the advisability of running back to Scrabster Roads. The master, however, decided to run on through the Pentland Firth, and in so deciding the Court are of opinion that he was guilty of the error of judgment which ended in the loss of the "Copeland." What led him to that decision does not appear from the evidence. If it was that the severe gales encountered had injured the hay, and that he doubted whether he would have sufficient provender for the ponies till Leith was reached; this is no sufficient reason for the course adopted. For at Scrabster Roads provender might have been obtained, or if that was impossible the ponies might have been landed there. From the log-book the ponies seem to have suffered severely on the passage, as 12 had died Those on deck must have been in the worst position.

Want of provender, however, is negatived by the evidence of the master and the owner, who depose that the supply was sufficient. Whatever the reason, the master decided to run on through the Firth, and on the departure of the pilot at 10.55 a.m. with telegrams, started the engines on full spend ahead, steering E. by S. (magnetic), there being no deviation on that point. The master kept on this course for forty minutes, by which time he thought the vessel had made about six miles, as her speed was 9 knots an hour. He further calculated that the current, which he estimated was running 6 knots an hour, must have carried him past the north end of Stroma. At 11.35 he altered the course to E.S.E. (magnetic) and reduced her engines to half speed, as the weather had become so thick they could only see about a length of the vessel ahead. This course was kept for ten minutes, i.e. to 11.45, when breakers were seen ahead and on the port bow, about the length of the ship off. The helm was immediately put hard-a-port, the engines stopped and reversed full speed astern, but too late to save the ship. She took the ground at 11.45 and remained hard and fast on the north-west end of Stroma Island. The cause of the disaster is clear. There was nothing like a tide of 6 knots an hour, on which the master had calculated. The vessel had never reached the north end of Stroma Island, but was a mile from it when the course was altered to E.S.E. and S.E. This course carried her right on to the north west end of the Island. In so dense a fog, and with strong currents running, it was impossible to verify the distance run from Dunnet Head, and the Court do not suggest that the master neglected any means open to him of verifying the distance run. The distance from Dunnet Head to the north end of Stroma Island is about 8¼ to 8½ miles, and the "Copeland" could have only made 7 or 7½ miles of this distance when her course was altered to the southward under the impression that the distance run (6 miles) and the allowance for tide (more than 3 miles) had brought the vessel to the eastward of the island. In point of fact she was still to the westward of the island by a mile when the course was altered to the southward, and this southerly alteration then brought the N.W. end of the island right ahead of the "Copeland;" owing to the denseness of the fog they were unable to see this till the vessel struck at 11.45.

Every effort seems to have been made to get the vessel off after she took the ground by reversing the engines to full speed astern; but finding it was impossible to move her, that the water was flowing into No. 2 hold, and the mainmast was lifted up about two or three feet, the boats were got out to land the passengers and crew. The passengers were landed by shortly after one o'clock. In the meantime eight or ten boats had pulled out from the east side of Stroma Island. Some of the passengers were landed in these boats and some in the ship's boats, and the water rapidly rising in the hold. The fires were drawn in the engine-room and safety-valves eased. Sea-cocks shut and banker-doors put down. Some fifty or sixty of the men from the shore were engaged to land the ponies. This they proceeded to do in the afternoon, and a certain number of the ponies were put overboard that day (the 25th), and swam on shore. But while the passengers and luggage were being landed the water had increased in No. 2 hold, till the ponies, which were in the lowest compartment of that hold, about 110 in number, were drowned. It is not clear by what hour all the 110 ponies in the lower compartment of hold No. 2 were drowned, but there is evidence that some of them were seen swimming in the hatchway between two and three in the afternoon. The ponies which were landed from the ship on the day she struck were taken from hold No. 1 and from the decks. There is no evidence that any attempt was made to save any of the

ponies from No. 2 hold. Had it been made it might have been found impossible to get the ponies out; but the Court are of opinion that if it was possible to land any ponies on the 25th July, an attempt should have been made to land those in No. 2 hold, which were in immediate danger, and that those in holds Nos. 1 and 3 should have been left till such attempt had been made. The ponies in holds 1 and 3 proved to have been in comparative safety on the 25th July, as they were safely landed on the 26th. As it was feared that the ship would break asunder during the next tide, all hands left her for the night at 6.30 p.m. The next day they commenced to land and save the remainder of the ponies. No water had come into No. 1 or No. 3 holds, but No. 2 hold was full up to the between decks, and the engine-room up to the platform. There seems to have been 482 ponies on board when leaving Iceland, 12 of which, according to the log-book, died on the voyage, and 110 were drowned in No. 2 hold, leaving about 360 as saved and landed on Stroma. The rest of the cargo, wool and fish, were also saved, and on the fifth day the vessel parted amidships. No lives were lost. All the witnesses examined on the point gave evidence as to the high character of the master as a sailor. His own evidence was clear and straightforward.

On the conclusion of the evidence the following questions were handed in by the solicitor for the Board of Trade:—

1. What was the cause of the stranding of the vessel?
2. What number of compasses had she on board, where were they placed, and were they in good order and sufficient for the safe navigation of the ship?
3. When and by whom where they made, and when and by whom where they last adjusted?
4. Did the master ascertain the deviation of his compasses by observation from time to time? Were the errors of the compasses correctly ascertained, and the proper corrections to the courses applied?
5. Whether proper measures were taken to ascertain and verify the position of the vessel about 10.15 a.m. on the 25th ult., and from time to time thereafter?
6. Whether safe and proper courses were set and steered after passing Dunnet Head, and whether due and proper allowance was made for tide and currents?
7. Whether, having regard to the thick state of the weather, the lead was used with sufficient frequency?
8. Whether a good and proper look-out was kept?
9. Whether every effort was made to save the lives of the live stock on board?
10. Whether the vessel was navigated with proper and seamanlike care?
11. Whether the master and officers are, or either of them is, in default?

It was added that in the opinion of the Board of Trade the certificate of the master should be dealt with.

Mr. Smith having addressed the Court, and Mr. Sutherland having been heard in reply for the master, the Court proceeded to give judgment on the questions upon which its opinion had been asked as follows:—

1. The stranding of the ship was brought about in the first place by too great a distance being allowed for the set of the tide, which was not by any means so strong as was supposed; and from the course being altered to the southward under the impression that the vessel had passed Stroma Island, whereas in reality she was still to the westward of it; and secondly, that owing to the thick weather the master was unable to verify the distance run from Dunnet Head, nor was he able to see Stroma Island until he was only a ship's length from it, and too late to be of any service.
2. She had three compasses—one placed on the bridge (called the standard) by which the courses were set, one placed in the wheel-house under the bridge, and one aft in front of the after steering gear; they were all in good order, and sufficient for the safe navigation of the ship.
3. They were made by Messrs. Whyte & Co., of Glasgow, at what date does not appear, and they were adjusted by the makers in May last.
4. The master ascertained the errors of his compasses from time to time on the previous voyage, but was unable to do so on this voyage, observations being unattainable on account of thick weather. There were no errors on the standard compass, excepting one degree only on the S.E. courses, which was correctly applied when steering those courses.

5. Proper measures were taken to ascertain the position of the ship about 10.15 a.m. on the 25th July, but owing to the thick weather and the uncertainty of the tide, it was impossible to verify the position after leaving Dunnet Head, and this led to her stranding.

6. The first course set was a safe and proper one had the weather been sufficiently clear to have seen Stroma Island, but as the vessel had not made sufficient distance on the first course to be clear of the north end of Stroma Island (and as there were no means of verifying the distance run on the first course on account of the fog) the subsequent alterations were made too soon, the master having allowed for more tide than there was in reality.

7. Up to making Dunnet Head the lead appears to have been used with sufficient frequency, but after that we do not think the lead would have been of much service in determining his position.

8. A good and proper look-out seems to have been kept, the master and mate being on the bridge, and a man on the forecastle head.

9. Vigorous efforts seem to have been made to save the ponies, and with the exception of those on the lower part of No. 2 hold and the 12 which died on the passage, they were almost all landed on Stroma Island. It appeared to the Court that after landing the passengers, the first effort should have been directed to ascertain whether it was impossible to save the ponies in the lower compartment of No. 2, as it was only in this hold that the water came in. But there is evidence to show that some, though not all, of these ponies may have been drowned whilst the crew were endeavouring to save, first the ship, and failing that, the lives of the passengers and themselves.

10. Up to arriving off Dunnet Head we have no doubt the vessel was navigated with proper and seamanlike care; but from that point we think the master acted imprudently in attempting to run through the Pentland Firth in such thick weather when it was impossible to verify the distance run.

11. The master is alone to blame for the casualty, and we are of opinion that in attempting to make the passage of the strait in such thick weather he committed a very grave error of judgment, knowing as he did, that there were no means of verifying the ship's position in a strong tide-way running at an uncertain rate, and where the lead could have been of little guide to him; however, taking into consideration his long service as master, the excellent character given him in court by the owners, and that there was no negligence attributable to him, but only an error in judgment, the Court does not deal with his certificate.

(Signed)   J. C. SHAIRP, Judge.

We concur in the above.

(Signed)   KENNETT HORE, } Assessors.
             EDWARD BROOKS, }

Edinburgh, 27th August 1888.

Wreck Report for 'Copeland', 1888

Unique ID: 15385.
Description: Board of Trade Wreck Report for 'Copeland', 1888.
Creator: Board of Trade.
Date: 1888. Copyright: Out of copyright.
Partner: SCC Libraries

TRANSCRIPTION

(No. 3599.) "COPELAND" (S.S.) The Merchant Shipping Acts, 1854 to 1876.

IN the matter of a formal Investigation held at the Sheriff Court House, Edinburgh, on the 24th and 27th days of August 1888, before JOHN CAMPBELL SHAIRP, Esquire, Sheriff-substitute of Mid Lothian, assisted by Captain KENNETT HORE and Captain EDWARD BROOKS, into the circumstances attending the stranding of the steamship "COPELAND," at Stroma Island, Pentland Firth, on 25th July 1888.

REPORT OF COURT.

The Court, having carefully inquired into the circumstances attending the above-mentioned shipping casualty, finds, for the reasons stated in the annex hereto, that the stranding of the steamship "Copeland" was caused by the master having allowed too much for the set of the tide, and having accordingly altered his course to the southward, under the impression that the vessel had passed Stroma Island, whereas she was in reality still to the westward of it. Further, the master was unable to verify the distance run from Dunnet Head owing to the dense fog which prevailed and the currents which were running. The Court is of opinion that the master committed a very grave error of judgment in attempting to make the passage of the Pentland Firth in such weather, but for the reasons stated they do not deal with his certificate.

Dated this 27th day of August 1888.

Â
(Signed)
J. C. SHAIRP, Judge.
We concur in the above report.
Â
(Signed)
KENNETT HORE,
EDWARD BROOKS,
Assessors.

ANNEX TO THE REPORT.

This was an inquiry into the loss of the British steamship "Copeland," held before John Campbell Shairp, Esquire, Advocate, Sheriff substitute, at the Sheriff Court House, George IV. Bridge, Edinburgh. Mr. Smith appearing for the Board of Trade, Mr. Sunderland for the master, and Mr. Kelly watched the case on the part of the owner.

The "Copeland," which forms the subject of this investigation, was an iron screw steamer of 438 tons register, and 798 gross tonnage, built in Govan in the year 1874, classed 100 A 1 at Lloyd's, and registered at the Port of Leith, her official number being 71,681. She was 225 ft. 3 in. in length, 29 ft. 3 in. in breadth, and 15 ft. 5 1/2 in. in depth, and at the time of the casualty was owned by James Gourley Bridges, Esquire, of No. 40, Shore, Leith, who was also the managing owner. She was rigged as a three-masted schooner, and fitted with two surfacecondensing compound engines of 150 horse-power combined, and had a passenger certificate from the Board of Trade to carry 566 passengers, and was engaged in the Iceland trade, running between Leith and Rigkjavik, and was also fitted to carry cattle. She had five boats of 878 cubic feet capacity, fitted with all requisites for use when last surveyed and inspected by the Board of Trade surveyor on the 13th June 1888. She had three compasses, one on the bridge (a standard), one in the wheelhouse under the bridge, a steering compass, and the third placed before the steering gear aft. They were all in good order and condition, and properly adjusted by Messrs. White, of Glasgow, in May 1888, who were also the makers of the compasses. The standard compass being correct magnetic on all points except six, viz.: E., E. by N., and E.N.E, S.E., S.E. by S., and S.S.E., even on these points there was only 1Â° of deviation. The "Copeland" was commanded by Mr. Charles Thompson, (who holds a certificate of competency as master, numbered 5,183), and had a crew of 30 hands all told, and eleven passengers when she last left Iceland. She was in every respect well found, and properly fitted and equipped for the voyage.

She left Rejkjavik on the 20th of July last with a general cargo consisting of fish, wool, and 482 ponies, bound for Leith, and her draught of water on leaving that place was 11 ft. forward and 15 ft. aft. She seems to have encountered very heavy N.E. and easterly gales after her departure, and her passage had thus been a long one up to the time of her making the land off Strathie Point. At this time the wind and sea had fallen, a dense fog had set in, with light easterly airs, and the ship's engines were put at half speed. On the morning of the 25th July, at 6 a.m., the fog lifted, and the second mate, who was then in charge of the deck, sighted, as he said, Strathie Point. A course was steered eastwards towards Dunnet Bay along the land, the vessel being stopped at times to take soundings. The master's object in taking these soundings seems to have been to make Dunnet Head, and so to get a good departure for running through the Pentland Firth. As the weather was so thick as to oblige the ship to proceed at half-speed, it seems to have been a very desirable and prudent course to take these soundings. But the Court are of opinion that, looking to the state of the weather when the "Copeland" made Dunnet Head, and knowing, as the master did, that the tides there run from 5 to 10 knots an hour, it was by no means a prudent thing to attempt the passage of the Pentland Firth in so dense a fog. How dense this fog must have been is proved by the fact that those on board the "Copeland" could not see the lighthouse on Dunnet Head when passing within half-a-mile of it; while the master states himself that when the ship struck on Stroma Island they could not see more than a ship's length a-head. To attempt the passage of the Pentland Firth under such conditions seems the more imprudent when it is remembered that the lead could have been of but very little use or the log either, when running in such a tremendous tide-way. And seeing that the principal thing required was an accurate knowledge of the distance run, and the course made good in passing through the Firth, it seems in the opinion of the Court that the best course would have been for the master to have remained in or off Scrabster Roads till the weather cleared sufficiently to make Stroma Island. Probably the ship would only have been detained a few hours by doing this. However, on making and passing Dunnet Head a fishing boat was sighted and hailed, the vessel stopped and boarded by the fisherman (or pilot as he called himself), and a telegram sent on shore to the owners. Some conversation seems to have taken place between the master and the fisherman-pilot as to the strength of the tide, the time it would run, and the state of the weather, and also the advisability of running back to Scrabster Roads. The master, however, decided to run on through the Pentland Firth, and in so deciding the Court are of opinion that he was guilty of the error of judgment which ended in the loss of the "Copeland." What led him to that decision does not appear from the evidence. If it was that the severe gales encountered had injured the hay, and that he doubted whether he would have sufficient provender for the ponies till Leith was reached; this is no sufficient reason for the course adopted. For at Scrabster Roads provender might have been obtained, or if that was impossible the ponies might have been landed there. From the log-book the ponies seem to have suffered severely on the passage, as 12 had died Those on deck must have been in the worst position.

Want of provender, however, is negatived by the evidence of the master and the owner, who depose that the supply was sufficient. Whatever the reason, the master decided to run on through the Firth, and on the departure of the pilot at 10.55 a.m. with telegrams, started the engines on full spead ahead, steering E. by S. (magnetic), there being no deviation on that point. The master kept on this course for forty minutes, by which time he thought the vessel had made about six miles, as her speed was 9 knots an hour. He further calculated that the current, which he estimated was running 6 knots an hour, must have carried him past the north end of Stroma. At 11.35 he altered the course to E.S.E. (magnetic) and reduced her engines to half speed, as the weather had become so thick they could only see about a length of the vessel ahead. This course was kept for ten minutes, i.e. to 11.45, when breakers were seen ahead and on the port bow, about the length of the ship off. The helm was immediately put hard-a-port, the engines stopped and reversed full speed astern, but too late to save the ship. She took the ground at 11.45 and remained hard and fast on the north-west end of Stroma Island. The cause of the disaster is clear. There was nothing like a tide of 6 knots an hour, on which the master had calculated. The vessel had never reached the north end of Stroma Island, but was a mile from it when the course was altered to E.S.E. and S.E. This course carried her right on to the north west end of the Island. In so dense a fog, and with strong currents running, it was impossible to verify the distance run from Dunnet Head, and the Court do not suggest that the master neglected any means open to him of verifying the distance run. The distance from Dunnet Head to the north end of Stroma Island is about 8 1/4 to 8 1/2 miles, and the "Copeland" could have only made 7 or 7 1/2 miles of this distance when her course was altered to the southward under the impression that the distance run (6 miles) and the allowance for tide (more than 3 miles) had brought the vessel to the eastward of the island. In point of fact she was still to the westward of the island by a mile when the course was altered to the southward, and this southerly alteration then brought the N.W. end of the island right ahead of the "Copeland;" owing to the denseness of the fog they were unable to see this till the vessel struck at 11 45.

Every effort seems to have been made to get the vessel off after she took the ground by reversing the engines to full speed astern; but finding it was impossible to move her, that the water was flowing into No. 2 hold, and the mainmast was lifted up about two or three feet, the boats were got out to land the passengers and crew. The passengers were landed by shortly after one o'clock. In the meantime eight or ten boats had pulled out from the east side of Stroma Island. Some of the passengers were landed in these boats and some in the ship's boats, and the water rapidly rising in the hold. The fires were drawn in the engine-room and safety-valves eased. Sea-cocks shut and bunker-doors put down. Some fifty or sixty of the men from the shore were engaged to land the ponies. This they proceeded to do in the afternoon, and a certain number of theponies were put overboard that day (the 25th), and swam on shore. But while the passengers and luggage were being landed the water had increased in No. 2 hold, till the ponies, which were in the lowest compartment of that hold, about 110 in number, were drowned. It is not clear by what hour all the 110 ponies in the lower compartment of hold No. 2 were drowned, but there is evidence that some of them were seen swimming in the hatchway between two and three in the afternoon. The ponies which were landed from the ship on the day she struck were taken from hold No. 1 and from the decks. There is no evidence that any attempt was made to save any of the ponies from No. 2 hold. Had it been made it might have been found impossible to get the ponies out; but the Court are of opinion that if it was possible to land any ponies on the 25th July, an attempt should have been made to land those in No. 2 hold, which were in immediate danger, and that those in holds Nos. 1 and 3 should have been left till such attempt had been made. The ponies in holds 1 and 3 proved to have been in comparative safety on the 25th July, as they were safely landed on the 26th. As it was feared that the ship would break asunder during the next tide, all hands left her for the night at 6.30 p.m. The next day they commenced to land and save the remainder of the ponies. No water had come into No. 1 or No. 3 holds, but No. 2 hold was full up to the between decks, and the engine-room up to the platform. There seems to have been 482 ponies on board when leaving Iceland, 12 of which, according to the log-book, died on the voyage, and 110 were drowned in No. 2 hold, leaving about 360 as saved and landed on Stroma. The rest of the cargo, wool and fish, were also saved, and on the fifth day the vessel parted amidships. No lives were lost. All the witnesses examined on the point gave evidence as to the high character of the master as a sailor. His own evidence was clear and straightforward.

On the conclusion of the evidence the following questions were handed in by the solicitor for the Board of Trade:

1. What was the cause of the stranding of the vessel?
2. What number of compasses had she on board, where were they placed, and were they in good order and sufficient for the safe navigation of the ship?
3. When and by whom where they made, and when and by whom were they last adjusted?
4. Did the master ascertain the deviation of his compasses by observation from time to time? Were the errors of the compasses correctly ascertained, and the proper corrections to the courses applied?
5. Whether proper measures were taken to ascertain and verify the position of the vessel about 10.15 a.m. on the 25th ult., and from time to time thereafter?
6. Whether safe and proper courses were set and steered after passing Dunnet Head, and whether due and proper allowance was made for tide and currents?
7. Whether, having regard to the thick state of the weather, the lead was used with sufficient frequency?
8. Whether a good and proper look-out was kept?
9. Whether every effort was made to save the lives of the live stock on board?
10. Whether the vessel was navigated with proper and seamanlike care?
11. Whether the master and officers are, or either of them is, in default?

It was added that in the opinion of the Board of Trade the certificate of the master should be dealt with.

Mr. Smith having addressed the Court, and Mr. Sutherland having been heard in reply for the master, the Court proceeded to give judgment on the questions upon which its opinion had been asked as follows:

1. The stranding of the ship was brought about in the first placeby too great a distance being allowed for the set of the tide,which was not by any means so strong as was supposed; andfrom the course being altered to the southward under theimpression that the vessel had passed Stroma Island, whereasin reality she was still to 1 he westward of it; and secondly, thatowing to the thick weather the master was unable to verify thedistance run from Dunnet Head, nor was he able to see StromaIsland until he was only a ship's length from it, and too late to be of any service.
2. She had three compasses-one placed on the bridge (called the standard) by which the courses were set, one placed in the wheel-house under the bridge, and one aft in front of the after steering gear; they were all in good order, and sufficient for the safe navigation of the ship.
3. They were made by Messrs. Whyte & Co., of Glasgow, at what date does not appear, and they were adjusted by the makers in May last.
4. The master ascertained the errors of his compasses from time to time on the previous voyage, but was unable to do so on this voyage, observations being unattainable on account of thick weather. There were no errors on the standard compass, excepting one degree only

on the S.E. courses, which was correctly applied when steering those courses.

5. Proper measures were taken to ascertain the position of the ship about 10.15 a.m. on the 25th July, but owing to the thick weather and the uncertainty of the tide, it was impossible to verify the position after leaving Dunnet Head, and this led to her stranding.

6. The first course set was a safe and proper one had the weather been sufficiently clear to have seen Stroma Island, but as the vessel had not made sufficient distance on the first course to be clear of the north end of Stroma Island (and as there were no means of verifying the distance run on the first course on account of the fog) the subsequent alterations were made too soon, the master having allowed for more tide than there was in reality.

7. Up to making Dunnet Head the lead appears to have been used with sufficient frequency, but after that we do not think the lead would have been of much service in determining his position.

8. A good and proper look-out seems to have been kept, the master and mate being on the bridge, and a man on the forecastle head.

9. Vigorous efforts seem to have been made to save the ponies, and with the exception of those on the lower part of No. 2 hold and the 12 which died on the passage, they were almost all landed on Stroma Island. It appeared to the Court that after landing the passengers, the first effort should have been directed to ascertain whether it was impossible to save the ponies in the lower compartment of No. 2, as it was only in this hold that the water came in. But there is evidence to show that some, though not all, of these ponies may have been drowned whilst the crew were endeavouring to save, first the ship, and failing that, the lives of the passengers and themselves.

10. Up to arriving off Dunnet Head we have no doubt the vessel was navigated with proper and seamanlike care; but from that point we think the master acted imprudently in attempting to run through the Pentland Firth in such thick weather when it was impossible to verify the distance run.

11. The master is alone to blame for the casualty, and we are of opinion that in attempting to make the passage of the strait in such thick weather he committed a very grave error of judgment, knowing as he did, that there were no means of verifying the ship's position in a strong tide-way running at an uncertain rate, and where the lead could have been of little guide to him; however, taking into consideration his long service as master, the excellent character given him in court by the owners, and that there was no negligence attributable to him, but only an error in judgment, the Court does not deal with his certificate.

Â
(Signed)
J. C. SHAIRP, Judge.
We concur in the above.
Â
(Signed)
KENNETT HORE,
EDWARD BROOKS,
Assessors.

Edinburgh, 27th August 1888.

LONDON: PRINTED FOR HER MAJESTY'S STATIONERY OFFICE, BY EYRE AND SPOTTISWOODE, PRINTERS TO THE QUEEN'S MOST EXCELLENT MAJESTY.

AND TO BE PURCHASED, EITHER DIRECTLY OR THROUGH ANY BOOKSELLER, FROM: EYRE AND SPOTTISWOODE, EAST HARDING STREET, FLEET STREET, E.C.; or ADAM AND CHARLES BLACK, 6 NORTH BRIDGE, EDINBURGH; or HODGES, FIGGIS, & Co., 104, GRAFTON STREET, DUBLIN. 1888.

Price Twopence.

54010-101. 375.-8/88. Wt. 23. E. & S.

SPONSORS:

Southampton City Council
New Opportunities Fund
Lloyd's Register
London Metropolitan Archives
National Maritime Museum
World Ship Society
Legal & Copyright
Screen Version

PARTNER SITES:

PortCities UK
PortCities Bristol
PortCities Hartlepool
PortCities Liverpool
PortCities London
PortCities Southampton

To

ROBᵗ SLIMON, ESQ.

& CAPT. JOHN COGHILL.

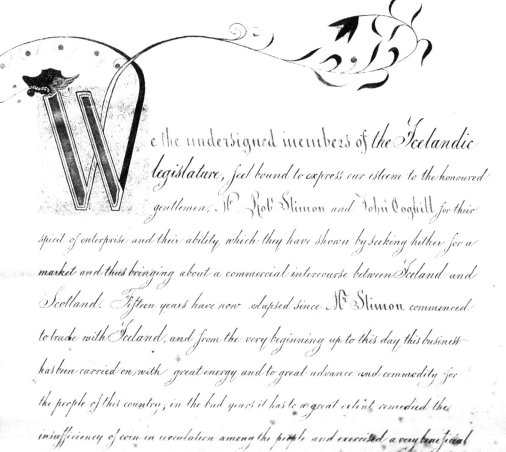

We the undersigned members of the Icelandic legislature, feel bound to express our esteem to the honoured gentlemen, Mʳ Robᵗ Slimon and John Coghill for their spirit of enterprise and their ability, which they have shown by seeking hither for a market and thus bringing about a commercial intercourse between Iceland and Scotland. Fifteen years have now elapsed since Mʳ Slimon commenced to trade with Iceland, and from the very beginning up to this day this business has been carried on with great energy and to great advance and commodity for the people of this country; in the bad years it has to a great extent remedied the insufficiency of coin in circulation among the people and exercised a very beneficial influence on the commerce at large, and it is for a great extent due to Mr Slimon's business, that, in large tracts of this country, the economical state of the people has not declined, nay, even made some progress; and it is commonly known and acknowledged and distinctly appreciated by our countrymen of what importance this trade of Mr Slimon's has been to their fortune and progress. This trade then has been of that laudable nature, as to be truly advantageous to both parts, no less beneficial to the Icelanders than to Mr Slimon himself.

But when we therefore now pay our respectful compliments to Mr Slimon as the originator and principal of this trade, we must with especial honour and thankfulness mention Mr Coghill, who for many years has been the agent and participant of the business, and whose energy, honesty, fairness and goodwill has won him a public confidence and popularity, and the high respect of all the many who have had commercial intercourse with him, and the beneficial results of all this business is therefore greatly due to him!

We therefore tender our best thanks to these honoured gentlemen for the commercial intercourse they have held with our country up to this date, and wish that the same may thrive and flourish in the future!

Reykiavík, 22. august, 1885.

Einar Ásmundsson, farmer.	Sighv. Árnason, farmer.	Jón Sigurðsson, farmer.	E. O. Kuld, provost.
Jakob Guðmundsson, clergyman.	Jón Pjetursson, chief justice.	Árni Thorsteinson, country treasurer, speaker of the united houses.	
L. Sveinbjörnsson, judge of the supreme court	Ásgeir Einarsson, farmer.	Skúli Þorvarðarson, farmer	
P. Pjetursson, bishop, speaker of the upper house.	F. S. Stefánsson, farmer.	Þorvarðr Kjerulf, physician.	
B. Sveinsson, sheriff.	Þórarinn Böðvarsson, provost.	Magnús Andrjesson, clergyman.	
Ólafur Pálsson, farmer.	Þorsteinn Jónsson, farmer.	Eiríkur Briem, professor of the Theol. College.	
Lárus Blöndal, sheriff.	Þorlákur Guðmundsson, farmer.	Jón Ólafsson, editor.	
Egilsson, merchant.	G. E. Briem, merchant.	Þorkell Bjarnason, clergyman.	
Grímur Thomsen, speaker of the lower house.		H. K. Friðriksson, vicepresident of the College.	

Printed in Great Britain
by Amazon

73737436R00106